THE DREAM

of Jack Love

D.W.HAGGARD

First Published in 2020 by Blossom Spring Publishing
The Dream of Jack Love Copyright © 2020
D.W.Haggard
ISBN 978-1-8380188-3-2
E: admin@blossomspringpublishing.com
W: www.blossomspringpublishing.com

Vos can pingere aliquid

List of Characters

Jack Love – 12 year old boy, great artist, visionary footballer
Millie Love – Jack's mother activist, teacher, leading artist
Charlie Love – Jack's father activist, teacher, artist, guitarist
Shirley Spinks – Jack's Nan, 61 years old, artist, philosopher, cleaner
Giagia – (Grandmother in Greek) the Tiger, Jack's jungle mentor and guide
Basakeira – the Killer Lion (brutality in Basque)
The Minstrel (sounds like Kate Bush) – saved by Jack and Giagia
The Snake Charmer – powerful philosopher

(uses Bolivian Siku pipes)

Captain Capstan non Filtre – evil jungle smoking man warlord – dries people

Professor Cringeworthy – Good Art college principle

Maurice Bosenquet – Cringeworthy's egotistical, social climbing successor

Keith Candice – TV presenter, shallow, mean bullying, egotistical

Mr Murray – 42 years old, kind-hearted, under 13s football coach Ashton FC

Mr Burns – 33 years old, artist, art teacher St Barnabys School

Fiona Casa Savoia – rich, hates Jack, self proclaimed Italian princess, artist

Tarquin Crassus – Genus (fat-type in Latin) aristocratic young artist

Crispin Newcash – extremely jaded wealthy Anglo-American young artist

St. John-Zedong Brown – privileged pseudo-Maoist young artist

Beatrice Crepitu – (crash in Latin) critical, west London socialite young artist

Gerald Formosa – weak Old Topcroftian central defender

Augustus Piano – aggressive Old Topcroftian central defender

Formaldehyde Tyke – spoilt Old Topcroftian

mid-fielder
Susan Hill – Kind and considerate Jack's friend and classmate
Maureen O'Sullivan – Jack's friend, classmate and supporter
Ben Stone – Jack's friend, classmate and Ashton FC striker
Dan Frindel – Jack's friend, classmate and Ashton FC striker
Steve Cowap – Jack's friend, classmate and Ashton FC striker
Tommy Grace – fifth year coward and bully
Wayne and Darren Webb – fifth year followers of Tommy Grace
Old Charlie – Woodford green grocer, Snakes Lane East
Stanley Onion – Old Topcroftians 'fixer'and conman
The Commentatoris – Queen Fiona's jungle assassins
The Moustachioed Man – Henri Rousseau

Chapter 1

From when Jack was four years old he had always liked the Central Line tube trains that rattled past his Nan's 1960s maisonette in Woodford. He didn't know why, he just did. He thought that it might have something to do with the big Underground Map his Nan had on the wall in the kitchen diner. The house was right by the station, next to the newsagent on the corner. From as far back as he could remember Jack liked to run his finger along the red Central Line on the map from Woodford, sometimes into London and out west as far as West Ruislip. Sometimes out of London, past Epping to Ongar. Over time Jack had worn a path onto the map, especially when he used a pencil to trace a journey. He knew the map of the Central Line off by heart, frontwards and backwards and sideways if you included the Hainault loop. He thought the map was a wonderful thing and it gave him comfort each morning when he heard the Central Line tube trains start their journeys as they made their little house shake at 5.30 a.m.

The kitchenette was a small room, twelve foot by ten foot, with a yellow Formica topped kitchen table in it, which opened up when they had their dinner. Jack had lived on his own with his Nan for as long as he could remember, he had no brothers or sisters. Just, Jack and his Nan. Jack's Nan seemed to him to be a quiet and reserved woman, almost timid, but not quite. Her name was Shirley Spinks or Shirl for short.

Nan's eyes were kind and caring, when she looked at Jack, they showed sadness. Jack imagined that if his Nan had been a house, it would be like when it was left in darkness, where just a soft landing light shone, cosy and comforting.

Jack's Nan kept the little house spick and span and it was a house of love and warmth, but there was something missing. In a time before Jack could remember, his mother and father had died. He had been told from a young age, that they were both killed in an industrial accident. He didn't know what and industrial accident was. When he got a little older he wondered what industry they were in. He saw a TV programme about the Industrial Revolution and then he pictured a huge steel foundry whenever he heard the word industry or a massive cotton mill factory like in the prints on his Nan's wall. There was one factory painting though, which had a different look and a different colour scheme. The perspective and scale seemed to be deliberately off, so that when you looked at it you felt giddy, like you were sliding off to one side.

His Nan's love was no longer concentrated on his mother and father but now on Jack instead. Jack's Nan had two jobs. She cleaned local offices and shops during the day and of a night time she painted boxes and boxes of toy soldiers on a piece rate for a local toy company. Nan was their best painter. The toy company's van would deliver ten gross of German infantry one week: ten gross of British Marines the next week. Nan had her system of painting each type of soldier. When they were painted Nan set them to dry on the kitchen table over night, after dinner. Jack helped paint the soldiers as well. He had very good control of the small brushes, painting belts, rifles, eyes and back packs with great skill. Jack's job was to keep the brushes in good order, cleaned with spirit each night, ready for the next evening.

"We are painters, you and I", smiled Jack's Nan, at least once a week.

Jack dreamed that one day he would

be a famous artist. He loved painting pictures, when sat at the kitchen table. He would use the toy soldier brushes to paint with Acrylic water colour paint, instead of the strong cellulose the toy company gave them. He would paint pictures and ideas onto the backs of card menus that his Nan brought home from a restaurant that she cleaned each week. The cards were A4 size. Jack liked to paint pictures of tube trains or of footballers from his local team, Leyton Orient. Jack liked Orient's goalkeeper Mervyn Day and the winger John Chiedozie, so he painted these two players the most.

He asked John Chiedozie to sign one of his paintings one day as John was coming off the field, after being substituted against Newcastle and to his delight he did! John wasn't happy about being subbed. Jack could see that. He signed Jack's painting though and asked him to bring another one to the next home game.

Nan's work, to keep food on the table, never stopped. As a result of this hard and relentless toil, Jack thought Nan always looked tired. They didn't have much money, but they had enough food to eat and Jack's clothes were washed and neatly ironed for when he went to school each day and his kit was always ready for football at the week-ends.

There were no photographs of Jack's mother and father in the house. One day Jack, when he was about ten years old, asked his Nan why this was.

"Where are the photos of Mum and Dad," asked Jack one Saturday evening, after they finished painting the boots of the

Africa Corps.

"We've only got that one, wedged in the frame of that beauty painting," remembered Jack.

Nan was busy again, now attending to the stewing a neck of lamb on the stove and was almost invisible behind the steam coming up from the big black saucepan.

"The photographs? They all got burnt Jack, we had a big clear out after the accident and they all went, I'm sorry love, oh, except for that one where they are pointing inland. You know the one."

Jack had distant memories of his mother and father. He remembered being with them in a great big green field and he could smell freshly cut grass, playing with a toy penguin. It was either a real memory or the memory of a photograph that he had then built up. Some nights Jack dreamed of his mother and father. The dream always went the same way. He would see them both sitting in a cafe, he would run down the street to meet them, only to see them turning a corner. He would then run to the corner and there they were getting on a 139 red Route master Double Decker bus, just out of reach, always just out of reach and not quite in focus. He would shout, "Wait! Wait!" they didn't wait, but they did sometimes wave back, he was never quite sure.

On Saturday nights Jack's Nan loved to play her records on an old Dansette record player in the front room. Jack went through the cupboard where the records were kept; there was record by someone called Chopin, which never got played, it was stacked in a pile at the back. He sometimes wondered about that record. It seemed out of place.

Nan's favourite record was by Marianne Faithful singing 'The Ballard of Lucy Jordan'.

Jack liked the song and asked his Nan one Saturday night, "What does suburban mean Nan; she says suburban in the song?"

Jack was curious as Marianne Faithful sang about suburbia in the song you see.

"Oh, that's a tricky one Jack. It means not a place in the countryside."

"Like Ongar," Jack interrupted.

"Yes Jack, like Ongar and not somewhere right in the big city. Some people think suburbia means a 'not some-where' place, a place 'between places', a 'nothing place'. I like suburbia Jack; it has many hidden and wonderful surprises that many high minded people often miss.

Because it is somewhere. Somewhere very real and very special indeed."

"So are we suburban people?" asked Jack.

"Yes we are, Jack, but that's no bad thing you know."

Nan then started to sing the bit in the song where the woman dreams of driving through Paris in a sports car with the warm wind in her hair. Nan's face always went a bit strange when she sang this part of the song. Jack dreamed of suburbia that night. He tried to remember the dream the next day but couldn't quite get it. All he could remember was it seemed very beige and his Nan was in it, being very beige.

On Tuesday evenings there was Jack and Nan's second favourite entertainment of the week, watching David Attenborough's

'Life on Earth' on BBC2. Jack and his Nan were transfixed one evening watching the 'First Forests' episode. Jack was fascinated by the idea of a jungle, untouched by man, where creatures evolved and developed, in the heat and the wet. Huge spiders hung in dew filled webs and colourful millipedes, David explained, ruled the roost. That night Jack dreamed of the jungle, the hot steamy jungle, filled with exotic creatures and animals. Not suburbia.

In the small postage stamp size of a garden was an old shed. It was painted dark with creosote. It was locked with two very large padlocks, securing the door with two hasps screwed onto the wooden structure. The windows were almost impossible to see through, with the dust, grime and spiders webs, covering them on the inside and outside. Jack sometimes would put his nose to the edge of the shed door. He could smell a strange smell, coming from the inside. It smelt a bit like the gin Nan had at Christmas or on the Queen's birthday or the spirit he cleaned the brushes with. Up high, right on the eaves of the shed was painted a strange eye, like the eye of a wild animal, almost too terrible and terrifying to behold. Jack used to imagine the shed was a kind of Viking ship and that the eye was painted onto the bow, to strike fear into the enemies of the Vikings. Behind the shed, right on the edge of the garden was a cherry tree. At the end of the summer Jack and his friend Dan, would climb up onto the roof of the shed. They would do this by standing on some wooden fruit boxes from the green grocer around the corner, old Charlie. They would wait until Nan went out shopping and then start their mission. Jack and Dan would scramble onto the main branches and pick the cherries. They would take it in turn, throwing the cherries down to the one standing on the ground with a big bucket. Jack's Nan would make dark cherry jam and share it with Dan's family, who lived round the corner.

On Saturday nights Jack watched Match of the Day with Des Lynam presenting. Jack loved that show and the new slow motion football film clips. Jack would watch the slow motion very carefully and would stand up and try and copy the striker's movement as he approached the goal, usually to score.

Chapter 2

On Wednesday nights Jack walked to Ashton Playing fields down the hill, next to the gasometers, where he would train with his friends Dan, Steve and Ben for Ashton FC under 13s. They were all good footballers. But Jack seemed to have an extra skill, to the other boys. It was as if he knew where the ball was going to go, like he could see three or four passes ahead. It made him look very fast as he was always in position either for a pass or to make a block or tackle, on the pitch. They were trained by their coach Mr Murray, a kind hearted good man.

Mr Murray sometimes said that they played like 'a load of monkeys' just chasing after the ball. But Mr Murray knew that they were better than monkeys really. Especially Jack. Ashton's biggest rivals were the Old Topcroftians, from Buckhurst Hill. Their youth teams were offshoots from the local public school, Topcroft. They had professional coaches, wonderful training facilities, with warm water showers and soap and fitness trainers as well!

At the end of last season, 78/79 the Old Topcroftians and Ashton FC were in the final for the under 13s Essex Cup. The final was to be held on the second Saturday of the

Whitsun holiday week. Jack had played very well all season, controlling mid field, breaking up opponents play, holding the ball up and putting his own players through on goal, with pinpoint passes through the defences. Jack scored with some long range shots or from free kicks, to add to his overall contribution.

Two weeks before the final there was a knock on the front door of Nan's maisonette. Nan went to the door. A man was standing there in a dark blue overcoat, his smart blazer peeking through. Jack looked at the man from behind his Nan. He recognised him from some of the matches.

The man announced, "I'm Stanley Onion and I am a scout from Tottenham, may I come in?"

Nan let Mr Onion in. Before she could

really answer, he took off his coat and then sat at the kitchen table like he owned the place. Mr Onion said that he had watched Jack a few times home and away this season and was very impressed with his abilities. Jack noticed that Mr Onion seemed to be sweating quite a lot. Nan asked him if he would like a cup of tea. He said that he would.

"We would like to make Jack an offer, Mrs Spinks. We want Jack to join our academy next season, all expenses paid," smiled Mr Onion, with a toothy expression.

"That sounds wonderful Mr Onion," nodded Nan, looking at Jack, but without that much enthusiasm. Nan didn't like Mr Onion, there was something about him.

"Even better Mrs Spinks, you have qualified for a holiday in Spain. You fly out to Barcelona on 17th May for a lovely week in the sun."

Jack knew about the Catalan city of Barcelona and the wonderful Nou Camp. Nan and Jack went on their holidays for a week every August to a nice boarding house called the White Castle in Worthing. Mr Onion was sipping his tea now and loosened his tie. Jack noticed that the blazer that Mr Onion was wearing did not have the Tottenham emblem on the breast pocket. He noticed that Mr Onion's tie was not Tottenham's either. Both were of a more local variety, Old Topcroftians. Nan thanked Mr Onion for this wonderful offer and showed him to the door promising to call him on the number he had given to them.

"He was from Old Topcroftians," observed Jack, "they don't want me to play on 24th May against them."

"I know," agreed Nan, "Let's make sure your team wins."

Nan told Mr Murray that Old Topcroftians had tried to knobble Jack with the holiday bribe, but that Jack loved his club and would never let them down. Nan saw that Mr Murray was very moved by this revelation. At training on the Wednesday before the big match on Saturday, Mr Murray took Jack to one side.

He told him, "I know what they tried to do to you son. On Saturday I want you to be your full self, for the club, for your Nan and for you."

Jack, Ben, Steve and Dan stayed behind after the main training had finished. Jack had some ideas he wanted to run through with his team mates. He had a plan on how to unlock the mean Topcroftian's defence. The main idea was how to get his team mates through the Topcroftian backline in one piece. Jack had developed three secret weapons, a delicious back spin chip for over the defence and onto Steve's right boot; a weighted through ball which when combined with Dan running dummies left Ben through for a tap in; and finally a ball from the wings with such whip and curve on it all Dan had to do was toe-poke it home. They practiced for an hour before all going home tired to bed. If anyone had been watching they could only describe the training session as flipping awesome.

Years later the people that watched that under 13s Essex Cup Final between Old Topcroftians and Ashton FC still talked about it. The most repeated comment was that Ashton FC's midfielder played like Glen Hoddle. He seemed to stop time when he was on the ball. By half time during the big match the Old Topcroftians manager and club chairman wanted to call it a day, saying that it was too cold, too rainy, too windy for the boys to 'fully express' themselves. The parents of the Old Topcroftians were complaining from the side lines and some started to come onto the pitch, like they owned it, they had paid enough money after all for their boys' sports.

But Jack had already expressed himself twice in scoring with a wonderful 20 yards volley and a glorious up and over free kick and had put through Ben, Dan and Steve onto goal. At Half time Ashton were 5 – 0 up. They went on to win 8 – 0. As they all came off the pitch Gerald Formosa , one of the back line for the Old Topcroftians stood in front of his father stamped his well fed foot on the grass and whined, "I shan't, shan't, shan't, ever play football again against the cheating peasants Daddy, I just shan't."

"Rugby is the gentleman's game after all," sulked Augustus Piano, as he drank some homemade lemonade. "These rough types need to be pitied really, they have nothing, just this bloody wasteland suburbia!"

Formaldehyde Tyke, the Old Top-croftian central midfielder could be seen punching his father repeatedly in the stomach shouting; "You see I told you, I should have gone to Eton you pathetic parent. Bloody Topcroft is junk."

'Mr Onion' had his photograph in the

Woodford Gazette a few weeks later as he had been sacked for cooking the books at the Old Topcroftians. The headline read, "Onion, from Turnpike Lane, shown Red Card by Old Topcroftians."

Jack generally didn't like noise and particularly noisy crowds. But with football it was something different. Jack loved football almost as much as his painting. He and the 'boys', Steve ,Dan and Ben went regularly to see Leyton Orient play at Brisbane Road, travelling from Woodford on the Central Line tube, with Dan's Dad, Trevor. Jack could h handle the crowds and noise at Orient, they were like a wall paper pattern to him and he was in the wall paper as well. Jack look forward to his pie at half time. Trevor smoked a pipe, filled with St Bruno Flake tobacco. It smelt nice on the tube train, it made Jack feel relaxed, them being all together. Lovely Saturdays.

Chapter 3

Jack was in the second year of his secondary school, St Barnaby's. Dan, Steve and Ben all went to the same school and were in his class. Jack's walk to the school only took half an hour. The school was set between Woodford and South Woodford tube stations and so walking was what was needed. Jack's favourite subject was Art, followed by English and Maths. The school didn't really go in for football. They had one outstanding player though, the goalkeeper, Griffiths. At school Jack loved Art.

In September a new Art teacher joined the school. He was called Mr Burns. He wasn't young and he wasn't old. But he seemed young and full of the zest of life when he taught Art. Jack looked forward to double Art each Thursday morning. He liked the smell of the Art room, burning incense, poster paint smell and in the winter he liked the clay smell and heat from the kiln room where the children's pots, sculptures and tiles were fired.

Mr Burns had only been at the school a couple of weeks when he said to his class, "Right, I've looked at the weather forecast and checked my weather station in my garden and, wonderful news. Next Thursday we are going to have a lot of *wind*."

At this point Mr Burns spun round on his heel and pointed at the boy Towler, who produced a loud and long belch.

He carried on, "Excellent Towler, yes. You see when the earth is heated up, it warms the air, gases, if you like and as you know when warmed air expands, there is an expulsion of warm gas and…."

Mr Burns again, spun round on his heel and with an urgent and serious facial expression pointed at Butler this time. Butler then produced slow, rumbling controlled flatulence, which seemed to gather pace into a tumultuous crescendo. Mr Burns appeared satisfied with both Towler's and Butler's practical and timely class demonstrations.

Jack was crying with laughter and could not speak. Butler must have come dangerously close to soiling himself, which added to the funny mini drama. Butler was pleased with recognition, red-faced with effort, but pleased.

"Wonderful timing. The impact on the jet stream is significant, especially as it passes over the tropics. This is happening now, so next week, next Thursday, we will be making kites," asserted Mr Burns with mock self-importance.

The big day came. On Thursday morning the cherry tree was bending over the fence, the wind was so strong. Jack gazed out of the window. Mr Burns had prepared strong paper, white cotton and bamboo sticks for the kites. He demonstrated to the class on the big table at the front how to splice the bamboo sticks together forming a cross. He then used the old cotton sheeting to stretch across the frame of the kite. He then cut the paper up into diamond shapes to hang on the tail. He then strung it together and showed the class how to paint an animal identity onto it.

Mr Burns painted the Japanese text for the TV series 'Monkey', 西遊記, onto the fabric, in red. It looked brilliant.

All the children set about making their own kites. Susan Hill's was the best in terms of secure construction, Maureen O' Sullivan's was exceptionally neat and carefully spliced together. Katie Devlin painted stripes on her fabric and tied the twine on tightly.

Jack painted the eye from the shed on his kite. Steve had made his tail pieces in red the colour of Leyton Orient. By lunchtime, they had all finished their work. Mr Burns led them all outside to the playing fields next to the school. The children all stood about fifteen feet apart, holding on tight to their kites.

"Come on now, loosen some of your twine, let them catch the wind and rise up," Mr Burns told them.

"Get ready, release and release."

All the children loosened their twine attached to the centre piece of the kites. The children stood with their back's to the wind and on the count of three all threw their kites into the air and watched them start to ride the air.

"Look how high Jack's one has gone already," sighed Susan.

"He's going to lose it, if he's not careful," laughed Towler, trying not to look like he was concentrating too much on not letting his kite go. They looked beautiful.

Other children and staff were watching through the classroom windows.

"Look at that silly so-n-so, what's that new fella's name? Burnt is it? He's out there being keen and committed and committed he should be. If he carries on like this he'll make us all look bad," groaned Mr Salisbury from the searing heat of the staff room.

"Come on, be brave Towler, every-one, start to let more twine out so that the kites soar and really fly. Can you feel how free that feels," yelled Mr Burns.

Higher and higher they went. To the Saturday fisherman in the group the tug on the twine from the kites, flying high above now, felt like the pull of a perch in the river Roding. They all looked so distant now; the children knew they were still there, but somehow remote, like they had almost left the earth. They stayed like this for twenty minutes, in silence.

"You've felt the breath of freedom out here, but come on in now its lunchtime," shouted Mr Burns above the noise of the gusting wind. The class started to haul the kites back down, by winding in the twine around a small stick each had in their hand. The kites slowly started to come back into view, to be used another day.

Jack just stood there looking at his distant kite. He could not bear to bring it back down to earth. When the next huge gust of wind hit the children and the trees around the edge of the field bent their branches, Jack let go. Mr Burns saw Jack do this but did not shout. He saw the look on Jack's face and understood.

By the time the autumn term had finished Jack had produced many paintings in his Art class. Not just of footballers and tube trains. He had started to think about David Attenborough's 'Life on Earth' programme. Jack started to paint the 'First Forests' from his mind's eye and they were very good. In the spring term Mr Burns organised an Art trip to the National Gallery. Jack knew that they would go on the tube from Woodford on the Central Line to Tottenham Court Road and change onto the Northern Line south to Charing Cross. Jack was not keen on the Northern Line. He liked the red horizontal of the Central Line.

The Art class were looking forward to the trip. On the Thursday morning they all set off. They got to the National Gallery at 11.00. Mr Burns asked the children to go around the gallery and to see the paintings, meeting back by the front door at 12.00. Each child had a sketch book and an HB pencil and a request from Mr Burns that they draw down any ideas or make notes that came into their minds from looking at the paintings. The boys had recognised some faces belonging to the Old Topcroftians as they entered; they thought that they must be on a school trip as well.

Dan asked, "Jack did you see, that Tyke is here, the one that tried to chop you down?"

"Yes, I saw him Dan, it didn't touch me on the pitch though, he tried, but missed," replied Jack.

After twenty minutes Maureen O'Sullivan was in a gallery room admiring the wonderful painting, 'The Ambassadors' by Hans Holbein the Younger. She had started to sketch the skull from the front of the painting, when a Topcroftian boy stood in front of her and produced a large string on dried nasal mucus from his nose and placed it on the face of the 'French Ambassador' and started laughing. He started to fish in his nose again for a second assault on the painting.

Maureen stepped forward and shouted, "Don't you dare," and slapped the boy's ear extremely hard. The boy happened to be Gerald Formosa, centre back for the Old Topcroftians. His ear went very red and he started to cry as he ran back to his teacher who was lecturing a small group of Topcroftians in front of a picture of Queen Victoria. He started to point at Maureen, but ten thought better of it.

Jack walked around the gallery with Ben, Steve and Dan. They all liked the Turner paintings especially 'The Fighting Temeraire', the smoke and clouds, with the new steam tug pulling the old war ship stuck in their minds. Jack then took a detour by himself, he wasn't sure why. He found himself in gallery room 43. He turned and then……then….. he saw it. He could hardly breathe. He was stood in front of something very special.

He was transfixed by Henri Rousseau's **'Surprised! Tiger in a Tropical Storm'**. The jungle seemed so real and unreal to him. Teaming with a kind of life. But the tiger and the tiger's eye were what caught him the most. The eye could have been the eye he had painted onto his kite, like the one on the shed in his Nan's garden.

Jack found himself sketching a jungle scene, not copying the one in front of him, but something different, with a winding path, not too obvious and weaving through the undergrowth. Jack lost track of time. His concentration was broken when someone shouted, "Come on Jack, we're all by the front door."

Jack felt that he had discovered something special in the gallery, a great artist, whose paintings he could see the wonder in and marvel at it. There was something else as well. He felt connected to this artist and the jungle.

As Jack walked across Trafalgar Square all he could think about was the tiger and the jungle. Just as Jack could see Mr Burns was almost by the entrance to the Underground, he bumped into a smartly dressed man with a moustache.

"I'm very sorry young sir," smiled the man with a foreign accent, bowing in the process, "those tropical storms are such a surprise aren't they?"

Jack thought that the man was winking at him, in a conspiratorial fashion, a bit like Long John Silver in the TV series of 'Treasure Island,' when he wanted Jim lad to do something. Before Jack could say anything in reply, the man was gone. Jack thought he must be imagining things. It was a bright sunny day, not a cloud in the sky, with a long shadow being cast by Nelson's Column across the square. Jack hurried over to where the others had gathered around the top of the stairs to Charing Cross tube station. Jack was discombobulated! Was he now imagining things now in broad daylight?

Then he remembered the painting again and that heavy, heavy rain, thrashing down onto the leaves and onto the stripy beast. Mr Burns was in his element, he could see that all of the children had enjoyed the experience of the gallery and were happily holding their sketch books with pride.

Jack, Steve, Ben and Dan all got off the tube train at Woodford and started to walk home. As they turned the corner to Jack's road they saw an odd looking butcher's horse and cart with what looked like sides of beef on the back, wrapped in muslin cloth trot past them. A man at the front of the cart was shouting, "Obtenez votre viande ici," and ringing a hand bell.

Dan observed, "That fella looks like he's in a fancy dress competition, or are they filming something round here again?"

Dan was thinking of a Second World War drama had been filmed in Woodford Bridge the previous year.

"What's that all about," questioned Ben pointing to the fence near Jack's Nan's maisonette.

All the boys started to blink, to make sure of what they were seeing. Jack saw a row of green parakeets sitting on the iron railing in the front garden. They were cawing and preening themselves, in a very calm and orderly fashion. Just as Jack was going to knock on his Nan's door she opened it.

"Hello Jack, hello boys", smiled his Nan, she was carrying a bowl of peanuts.

"These nice birds have flown all the way from Africa I am sure, so the least I can do is give them their tea."

And with that, Jack's Nan laid out the peanuts on a metal Lyons cake tin lid on the path.

"Lots of funny 'stuff' about today Nan," noted Jack as he waved goodbye to his mates and walked into the hallway, "foreign men with moustaches going on about tropical rain, parrots at home on the fence and old fashioned horse and carts roaming about".

Quite peculiar, Jack thought.

"Did you see anything at the National Gallery that you liked?" asked Nan.

"Yes, there was this painter, called Rousseau. His tiger in the jungle, really hit me, just something about it."

Nan listened very closely to these words, her eyes focused keenly, deep in thought.

"That's nice then Jack."

"Do you want a cup of tea Nan?" asked Jack.

"Yes please Jack," answered Nan shutting the front door.

Jack made the tea and went to the fridge to get the milk out.

"What's that in the fridge Nan?" asked Jack, pointing to a new fruit siting on a saucer in the fridge.

"Oh that?" replied Nan, "Old Charlie gave me that in the greengrocers today and said it was for you to try and have a taste of the jungle. It's called a mango."

Jack had the mango after his dinner. He cut it carefully in half, for himself and his Nan. He carefully cut and scooped out the flesh into two Willow Pattern desert bowls. He bit into it. He thought it tasted wonderful, fresh like a peach and tangy like a pineapple.

Nan liked it as well, "This is nice Jack, I think I'd like the jungle if you eat this all day long," she laughed.

The next day, Friday, after school, Jack walked under the subway beneath the station to Woodford Broadway; he then turned left up Snakes Lane West to the Library. He knew Mrs Pettifor the librarian in charge of the reference section. She was seated at her desk with a blue microfiche machine in front of her. She was holding a thin blue square of acetate film up to the light and what was that in her hair, was she wearing a feather from a peacock or a bird of paradise? Jack wasn't sure, but it looked nice.

"Fancy seeing you here today Jack," Mrs Pettifor exclaimed, "no training tonight?" Mrs Pettifor was Mr Murray's married sister.

"No training tonight Mrs P. I have come in to look through some of your art books, on an artist called Henri Rousseau," answered Jack.

"Oh, that's a coincidence, do you mean this artist," and with that Mrs Pettifor pointed to a display and book collection all about Jack's favourite artist, that's why I am wearing this lovely feather."

The library shut at six thirty on Friday evenings. Jack went through the two big books on Rousseau, full of big colour plates. He was particularly taken with a painting called 'The Snake Charmer.' Jack had filled ten pages of his sketch book, with notes, drawings and rough shaded textures. Some of his work looked like snakeskin, some exotic leaves from a far distant jungle plant. Jack thanked Mrs Pettifor and went home for his tea. It would be fish and chips tonight from Broadway Fisheries and Poulterers, although no poultry would be required that night.

Thursday's double art with Mr Burns came around again very quickly. They were all in the art room, with their sketch books in front of them, full of drawings from the art trip. Ben, Dan and Steve had made some very good sketches of Turner's ships and boats and talked about why they had been interested in his paintings. Mr Burns asked them some questions.

"What's happening in that picture Steve?" asked Mr Burns talking about 'The

Fighting Temeraire'.

"Well sir, the old heroic sailing ship has had its day and its being towed in by the new steam tug. So it's a bit sad, but also respectful to a ship and its men for years of work, well done," answered Steve seriously.

"Thank you or that Steve. Very well thought out and observed."

"What do you have Maureen," asked Mr Burns.

"I have sketched a skull and a scoundrel," answered Maureen, "the skull is based on something from Holbein's painting and the scoundrel is from real life."

Mr Burns didn't ask too much about the boy with the red ear in the sketch (Maureen had added in some water colour). Dan thought he recognised this character from somewhere. "I like this Maureen you've 'caught' him very nicely, I would say," grinned Dan knowing Maureen knew he was in on the joke.

It came to be Jack's turn. He had painted this water colour, but with strong acrylic colours, on his kitchen table. The rest of the children and Mr Burns automatically stood up and walked and gathered around the painting.

"Look what he's done," smiled Maureen as she leant in to have a closer look, "it's great Jack."

It was a painting of Woodford Station, looking from Snakes Lane East. The news-agent on the corner, on the left, was there, Christoff's the barbers, Old Charlie's greengrocers on the right was there, with all the fruit laid out nicely.

Ripper had an interested expression on his

face, not normal for Ripper in Art.

"OK. Finally something I can under-stand, I can recognise all these bits he's put in the picture. Nice one Jack, nice one son." Ripper usually had a West Ham scarf tied round his wrist at all times, which impeded much of his school work, so this was a rare involvement from the boy with the long leather coat. Some of the class started chanting, 'Nice one Jack, nice one son', until Mr Burns arched his not insignificant eyebrows.

"It looks hot in the painting, look at the fancy birds," smiled Maureen, "I'd like to go there for my holiday."

Mr Burns asked the class to, "Look closely and see what Jack has invented. For it is an invention of his mind. He has found a freedom in his painting and put it down on this sugar paper."

The red brick on the Central Line Station was captured with flair and a rare skill. It was beautifully painted. But that wasn't all. It was painted as if Woodford had been transplanted to a version of the jungle, mostly like the Congo. There were parakeets in a line along the edge of the station, instead of pigeons, Jungle vines hanging down at the side framing the image and an antelope eating a piece of fruit from Old Charlie's , the greengrocers, hand. There were snakes hanging off the Snakes Lane East road sign, with their forked tongues testing the Woodford air.

"This is wonderful Jack," congratulated Mr Burns, "beautiful work, almost magical."

Maureen sighed, "Jack, you have

made us see something different, it's where we live, but so………, so exotic, yes that's it, so exotic, like a rare flower or bird."

At the end of the lesson Mr Burns asked Jack to remain for a moment as he had something to tell him. Jack waited back at his seat by his usual high table.

"Well Jack, I have some good news for you here," smiled Mr Burns with a glint in his eye as he handed Jack a letter.

"What's this sir," asked Jack.

"I have recommended you to be our school's representative artist to attend the Prince's Saturday Art School, in west London," answered Mr Burns, "it is a great honour and you will meet other young artists and work with Professor Cringeworthy at the art school."

"Thank you sir, is it near a tube

station?"

Jack was excited, but a little worried. He was only used to mixing with his friends around Woodford. He didn't mix with the children like in the Sunday afternoon TV series 'The Phoenix and the Carpet,' full of kids with nurseries, nannies, tennis rackets and flannels. He didn't dislike these TV posh kids, he just didn't know any. Jack thought some more.

"It will be for posh kids sir, won't it?" asked Jack.

"It's about art Jack, that's what matters nothing else and you are an artist, so off you go if you don't mind. It starts in a couple of weeks," said Mr Burns, "please get your Nan to sign the slip and return it to me tomorrow please."

"Thank you sir," said Jack.

It would be the end of the season by then so Jack would not be missing any matches. On the way home that night Jack wished that he had been more grateful to Mr Burns for thinking of him. He would make it up to him by doing his best art when he got to the Saturday School.

Chapter 4

It was Saturday 17th May, a week after the FA Cup Final, where West Ham had beaten Arsenal 1 – nil. It was also the start date for the Saturday School. Jack had packed his yellow Gola sports bag with some of his work brushes, a few fine brushes from Mr Burns, his sketch book and a set of new soft pencils from his Nan, in a tin.

Nan called out, "Mind how you go Jack," as she tied up her apron. Jack closed the front door behind him.

Jack checked the clock on the station platform for the time. He needed to be at the art school for a 9.00 a.m. start. Jack changed at Holborn on the Central Line onto the Piccadilly Line south to Knightsbridge. Jack had been to Knightsbridge before, as he and

Steve had visited the 'Way In' at Harrods to listen old Small Faces records that they still had in stock.

Jack was holding the map of where the art school was located, which had come with his letter.

"Can you tell me where this art school is please," smiled Jack as he spoke to a busy shopper, outside the station.

She looked at Jack with an annoyed expression, with sparks almost coming off a pair of speeding red patent leather shoes, "OK, OK, don't crowd me, go over there, then there, then there, then…..OK?"

Jack shrugged, "Thank you," and walked on.

"What, that's it, just one 'thanks'? You people are all the same."

He headed for 26 Lennox Gardens, a

tall red brick mansion building, with five steps leading up from the pavement.

As Jack turned the corner he could see a few cars parked outside number 26 on the pavement. They seemed to be competing on who could get the closest to the entrance of the building.

A dark green Range Rover was sounding its horn at the car directly in front of it, a red Jaguar sports car.

Jack could hear a girl screaming, "If I'm not the closest to the door I shan't go in and the Prince will have to find himself another royal artist. I shan't, shan't, shan't."

"Fiona darling, please just be satisfied, we are seven or eight steps to the main entrance of the art school, what more could you possibly want my precious," sighed Fiona's harassed father.

"S.A.T.I.S.F.I.E.D – are you mad? You are such a failure, my face will wrinkle up and cry forever, you failure, you fat, fat failure father," shouted Fiona.

"Look at all of your new brushes and paints and crayons and pastels and parchment and vellum and…………….."

"Shut up, it's all junk and useless if I'm not going in," she sneered as her lip pouted to a degree that would make the Guinness Book of Records for lip pouting, if there was such a category, which there wasn't.

Jack stood on his heels and watched. The green Range Rover edged forward and pushed the Jaguar backwards, into Mercedes, into a BMW and finally into a Bentley. The Jaguar owner got out of his car and marched forward banging on the bonnet of the Range Rover with his fists as he made for the driver's window.

"See here you buffoon, are you some form of ignoramus?" exclaimed the Jaguar man. Jaguar man's son, Crispin got out of the low car and with a small wooden artist's box sprinted in the direction of the main door.

Fiona was panicked by this spirited sprint for the door by Crispin, as she wanted to be first inside.

And with that all of the car doors opened and a variety of children and adults all spilled out and rushed for the front door in a flurry. There was pushing and shoving and a jam of people at the entrance. One fat woman in a grey tweed suit did actually seem to be jammed in the mahogany door frame.

"Perkins, give me a push through you lump of expensive lard," gasped the fat woman.

The uniformed driver so instructed needed to place his shoulder to her back to get her through the door frame. He huffed and puffed and pushed her in, losing three silver buttons from his tunic on the way. Jack saw them roll on the pavement, in a little arch and then down a drain.

"Forbes, give Tarquin his tureen, he must have his tureen or he will simply die of starvation," blubbered Tarquin's mother who had emerged from the dark blue Bentley and was issuing instructions to her chauffer. Tarquin's chubby little hand was being dragged forward by his father in an attempt to stake a claim to be among the first to be admitted to the Prince's art school.

Fiona was still yelling, "Let me pass, let me pass," whilst she clutched her leather art bag full of the most expensive paints made from the ground shells of rare birds, as she disappeared inside.

"Look father, bloody St John is here. I told you I never wanted to see him again after that boring polo match, can't you fix anything. Mummy is right you are absolutely useless," complained Fiona.

The cars were all parked this way and that, on the pavement, blocking the road. It was quite a sight. A parking attendant was now making her way towards the selfishly parked cars. The Range Rover was now the closest car to the entrance Jack noted. All the children and adults had gone inside. Jack held his Gola bag tightly and followed them through.

A middle aged man in a grey suit, who Jack took to be Professor Cringeworthy, was issuing instructions.

"Stand back, will you," as he gasped pitiful instructions to the unruly bunch of parents and children pushing and shoving in front of him.

"This will really not do, do you understand. Parents, please go outside now. Your line of demarcation is the front door. Off you go now," asserted Professor Cringeworthy.

A woman in a blue suit and pearls said, "Gerard, don't let this teacher speak to us in that way." As she said this she stamped her feet on the parquet flooring marking into with her stiletto heels.

"You have such wonderful manners madam, would you kindly remove yourself from the premises, it is rubbish collection day in Kensington and Chelsea so be as so kind to deposit yourself by the bins," instructed Professor Cringeworthy archly.

Jack laughed at this and in doing so caught Professor Cringeworthy's eye. The professor could see that he was the only child who had come alone and his face seemed to soften at this realisation.

"Ah, our artist from Woodford, come this way dear boy," said Professor Cringe-worthy as he pushed aside the grappling parents, "Make way, for the boy," said Professor Cringeworthy.

"Who is this unmentionable," stutt-ered the tweed suited woman, as all the faces turned towards Jack.

The other children immediately hated him as he walked steadily through the entrance hall, first left then right into the main studio, which was set up with five different work areas for the children.

Jack started to unpack his Gola bag at the position near the front of the class. He could still hear shouting coming from the lobby as the other children started to make their way into the room. As the children walked in the professor noted that they were dressed in what could only be described as 'in a uniform way'. The 'way' being how European rural peasants dress could be considered a uniform, expensive deliberately worn clothes. It looked as if they were attending a village meeting in rural France or a baker's convention in Tuscany.

Jack was wearing his best jeans, ironed by his Nan and his Solatio shoes with leather soles, which he had bought with the money from painting a gross of red Indians, at Beta-fit in Ilford.

Professor Cringeworthy gathered the children around the front of the studio on stools, to introduce themselves. He had rehearsed two ice breaker questions that he intended to ask each student in turn.

"Which of you is Beatrice Crepitu?" asked Professor Cringeworthy.

Before Beatrice could answer Fiona erupted saying, "I am an Italian princess and I should go first in everything, everything prof, got it!"

"With such majesty, as yours, I am sure you will be able to allow Beatrice to continue," sighed Professor Cringeworthy with raised eyebrows.

Professor Cringeworthy continued with his ice-breakers.

"Beatrice where did you holiday this year?"

Beatrice stood up and walked in front of Fiona so that she blocked out everyone's view of that girl.

"Well, this year we took a villa on the Amalfi coast for a month and then two weeks by Lake Como in a waterside hotel, owned by Omar Sharif. Mother and Father are in Omar's bridge team. It was simply divine. The locals did smell somewhat, like the goats, but you got used to it," dreamed Beatrice.

"Thank you dear," Professor Cringeworthy responded, "and who is St John-*Zedong* Brown?"

A boy wearing an olive green peasant's work clothes put his fist into the air.

"I see. Have I placed the hyphen in the correct place, you are St John-Zedong, surname Brown?"

"That is correct comrade. Brown has such utility one can smell the earth attached don't you think, the good earth of the Mekong Delta. and our leader has loaned me his inspirational name. Oh and I love the odour of goats."

"I don't understand you are not called Elizabeth are you, for her majesty is our leader dear boy, this is England in case you have forgotten," said Professor Cringe-worthy. "Where did you holiday, by the Great Wall?"

"Don't be silly, Prof, we generally head for Zurich, Daddy likes to catch up with his gnomes, but this year we slummed it in 'ol Biarritz."

"Where do you live?" asked Professor Cringeworthy.

"Oh, in a drab part of East Fortune Green," replied St John-Zedong.

"You mean Hampstead," questioned the Professor archly.

"What about Crispin Newcash, where are you please?" asked Professor Cringeworthy.

"That's Nuke-Cosh, you fermented prune. and before you ask, New York, Upper Manhattan and then to the Hamptons. We have horses there and a stud farm," neighed Crispin.

Crispin had a mid-Atlantic drawl to his accent. Professor Cringeworthy was starting to feel the onslaught from this collection of young artists.

The professor pointed at another young artist. A rotund boy in dark blue dungarees and Dr Martens boots and a red bandanna put his hand up and the professor nodded without speaking.

"I'm Tarquin Crassus-Genus; we vacate to south East Asia each year, to brush up on all that the great Buddha has to offer and all that lark," lisped Tarquin.

Each of the children had an accent which they seemed to sharpen on each other, with every word that they uttered.

"Ahem, ahem," shouted Fiona, with a growing crescendo.

"Go ahead young lady," murmured Professor Cringeworthy, feeling suddenly tired.

"AS I WAS SAYING I am an Italian princess, in fact THE Italian Princess of the

Casa Savoia," opined Fiona, who paused and then seemed disappointed that the gathered group didn't look impressed.

She continued, as she felt a further explanation was required, "That's the House of Savoy, to you riff raff."

"What 'Savoy' like the cabbage? You are named after a cabbage," laughed St John-Zedong, who seemed to detest Fiona and enjoyed baiting her. "You do look like a cabbage."

"That's enough, we want to get some painting done, so move on," instructed the professor with a wave of his hand as he turned on his stool and faced Jack.

He said, "You must be Jack Love, what have you got to tell us?"

"I live in Woodford, on the Central Line and my Nan and me go on our holidays to Worthing each year, to Mrs Braithwaite's bed and breakfast. "It's called The Dun roaming Castle on the sign outside."

"That's very nice down there Jack," smiled the Professor kindly.

"Yes. The Downs are not far and we walk a bit when we are there. We camp at Debden Green in Epping Forest as well, as it's so near to Woodford" Jack informed him.

Up to that point all of the other children had been competing with one another. Now, they turned as one on Jack and pointed and laughed at him, after all, the professor had led him in first, like he was special or something?

"You go to Worthing, what a pleb you must be. What is a Nan by the why, do you have it for supper?" laughed Fiona.

Jack's face reddened.

Chairman St John Zedong joined in and asked, "Do you live in caves in Woodford, it must be so, so backward, not like East Fortune Green. They live like 'The Moorlocks out there, in blasted caves. You want to live in East Fortune Green it's like a socialist republic where I live, with civilised people. Everyone in the party is there, Dobsbawm, Elitebrand, Boot. Why is this fascist here anyhow, anyone?"

Fiona called out, "Look at his clothes. What a fascist."

"Desist, desist, you are so tiresome and boring" instructed the Professor as he continued to halt these proceedings by waving his arms and then putting his hands up. He directed his students back to their tables and easels.

At that moment a man wearing a brown cotton coat came into the studio.

"This is Frank," smiled the Professor, "he is our very valuable and wonderful technician. He's here to help us with materials and any technical help in the production of the art that we will produce." Frank stood to the side as the professor continued.

"Tell me why you are interested in art Jack," asked Professor Cringeworthy with a genuine expression of interest.

"He doesn't know anything about art, none of them do," sneered Fiona folding her arms in a huff.

"How long have you been painting?" asked Cringeworthy?

"For as long as I can remember and then I paint for money, you know painting soldiers and animal figures," Jack paused, "it's called 'homeworking, you do it for big companies like Tompkins".

"See he paints soldiers, he's a fascist," yelled St John, "paints the shiny jack boots."

"Quiet, quiet," snapped Cringeworthy.

"Where do you paint," asked Cringeworthy?

"I sit by the kitchen table and me Nan and me do our painting," replied Jack.

"Isn't it difficult in such cramped conditions to produce art?" asked Cringeworthy?

"I don't think about art, just painting, I love it. When I paint I feel free, like I am a flying bird. and when I don't paint it's like I've landed on the ground, waiting for the moment to fly again," answered Jack with honesty.

"How did you learn how to paint," asked Cringeworthy?

"I don't know, trained m'self I suppose, I can't remember. Think it were difficult, but it might have been just at the start," thought Jack.

Jack's face had become animated when he spoke about painting. It was the same animation when he played football.

"You talk like a real artist Jack. It's like you become art when you are working," said Cringeworthy, "that's great to feel that way."

Jack's face was still, listening, but not saying anything.

"What brushes do you use Jack?" asked Cringeworthy.

"When the school throws out their old Winsor and Newtons each summer I collect them up. Nan and me go through them and throw out the bent or hardened ones. Those that's left we soak in a special spirit which Nan's got and we then use a fine wire brush to condition each brush back better than new," answered Jack, "kind of waste not want not."

"Thank you for telling us that Jack," replied Cringeworthy, with interest.
The Professor then set them their artistic challenge of the day.

"I want you to produce a piece of art which expresses your identity. Something about you, as a young person, a young artist. A view of your world. You have until three this afternoon," and with that Professor Cringeworthy pointed at the clock high up on the wall.

"Keep an eye on them with me Frank,

if you would and help out as needed please."

All of the children got started on their work. Fiona got busy with her new and rare pastels. St John-Zedong used a combination of charcoal and Japanese calligraphy pens to produce a range of forms.

"Do you see these pens Frank? They are made by Priest Gorō Masamune, swordsmith to the great samurai. They cost more than you earn in a year!"

St John-Zedong started to draw a long black line with his Masamune pen. As he pressed the nib down too hard it snapped, spaying ink all over St John-Zedong's face and expensive old clothes.

"You sure they're not from Woolworth's son?" asked Frank with a laugh.

Tarquin had opened a box of beads, rice and split peas and started sticking these to his paper with glue.

"Glue, glue," ordered Tarquin clicking his fingers at Frank, not using Frank's name in his ugly address.

Frank went to fetch the PVA glue from the cupboard and gave it to Tarquin. Tarquin snatched the plastic tube from Frank's hand a squirted a huge mound of white glue onto the table top and under the sleeve of his shirt.

"You know what happened to the little boy who didn't learn to say please," joked Frank with a wink, "he got stuck!" Crispin was using large mop brushes with different inks to get his effects, whilst Beatrice started on a very careful and fussy water colour. She hummed a tuneless tune under her breath, her life trainer had told her to this to balance her chakra. Frank watched

Jack start, there was something about this boy. Jack started his work with some rough sketching. He then switched to his strong coloured acrylics.

"What are you painting there?" asked Frank.

"Oh, it's the new tower block in Tamar Square, in Woodford."

Frank had not seen anything like it.

"What's it got all over it, you know up the sides, n'that?"

"This is the jungle. A concrete tower in a jungle thick with vines and creepers."

Frank could see greens of all shades, splashes of strong yellow sunlight cascading in creating deep shadows. He was impressed and mystified. The other children were whining so he had to go off and get what they all wanted.

Time flashed by and in what seemed like the blink of an eye it was lunch time.

Jack found himself sitting and talking with Frank. Frank had not had a chance to speak to Jack since her briefly looked at his work earlier in the morning as the other children had been demanding his attention, his fetching, carrying, mixing and fixing. Frank was said how much he liked Jack's painting.

"What's this all about then Jack?" asked Frank pointing to Jack's painting, "I can see what it is, but why?"

"Well, I like where I live in Woodford, it's nice, but sometimes I like to imagine its set in the jungle, like a lost city that you sometimes hear people finding in South America or somewhere."

"I know what you mean Jack. I live in

Buckhurst Hill, in Princes Road, where it backs onto Knighton Woods. There is a very old rockery there by a pond, part of the garden of a big house in the past, which is like a lost city as all the forest trees and shrubs have grown all over it now," smiled Frank with drama on his face.

Frank made Jack a cup of tea. The other children had gone to a restaurant around the corner to the art school. The professor had gone to his office, in the corner of the studio and was listening to the test match. Jack recognised Brian Johnston's voice in the distance. Jack heard a sound from the side of the room and he got up from talking to Frank to see what it was. He walked around the screen dividing that part of the room and found Fiona at St John's easel messing up his materials.

"Oi, stop that Fiona, leave his stuff alone," shouted Jack.

"What do you care, we all hate you anyway?" shouted Fiona, as she quickly made her way to her seat.

And with that the rest of the children filed in.

"Look what he's done," fumed St John pointing at Jack, "you really are low life, you are."

Professor Cringeworthy stood by Jack's side.

"Did you do this boy?" he asked.

"No professor, I stopped her," answered Jack quickly.

The Professor looked at Frank, he shook his head to indicate that it was not Jack's doing.

"Who was it Jack?" asked Professor

Cringeworthy.

Jack would not say who had messed up St John's stuff. But he looked at Fiona to see if she would own up. She didn't. and she didn't seem to care about what she had done.

Three o'clock came around quickly. The children were asked to assemble their work at the front of the class on the tables or easels. The Professor asked each student to introduce their work and started with Fiona, as he was getting tired and was not sure that he could take another load of shrieking from this girl.

"Well professor let me read you this letter from my mother published in today's Guardian. It's called 'Death from Suburbia'. It's what I've called my work this afternoon."

Fiona read her mother's letter where

she harangued and berated the thick suburbanites of London, for causing the election of a fascist Mayor. In the letter she compared the suburbanites of London to the Morlock cave dwellers of H.G. Wells' 'Time Machine', except that they had better personal hygiene in her view and a better diet. Not so many chips.

"So, my work is an attack on the plebeian oiks and their semi-detached lives," concluded Fiona, showing her violent pastel strokes.

A green parakeet flew into the room and perched on one of the beams dividing the triangular roof section of the large studio. It peered down for a while and seemed to be looking for something. Or was it someone? After a minute it flew down and bit Fiona's little finger on her right hand, squawked and flew off out of the window.

Frank thought he heard the bird say, "Fake, fake, fake," as it flew off into the distance. Fiona cried, drawing a sympathetic smile from Jack. No one else seemed to be bothered about her and they continued.

Jack went last and talked clearly and powerfully about his work and its meaning. Frank and the Professor could see the clear talent in this boy as he showed the 'Tamar Tower' as he called it, jungle vines and all.

"It's a jungle, a suburban jungle, full of light and dark, shadow and movement. The ebb and flow of the tube trains on their tracks. The flood of commuters, like some great river in flood at the end of every working day. No caves as far as I have seen though!"

To finish of the day the Professor

asked each student to talk about their favourite artist. St John-Zedong started the proceedings off.

"For me it has to be Vietnamese painter Le Pho, his passion, under the oppression of the western boot, for his art is incredible and moving," wafted St John's well practised lies.

Beatrice said, "I choose Georgia O'Keefe, her flowers are lovely. We have her pictures all over the house and in the orangery. She is simply splendid and no mistake."

"Only the Americans can make art now. It's got to be Barnett Newman," asserted Crispin, "he comes to our farm in the summer and he can paint stripes full of meaning, like no other."

"I love Freud. My mother loves

Freud. She poses for him in our house in Southwold. He says we are his second family. My father buys all his art, literally all of it. It's great. It's wonderful. It's in our basement in town," noted Tarquin, with new questions arising in his mind.

"There is only one artist. Its Picasso," insisted Fiona, "we have some of his work in our house at Como, he lived and created with a passion. He's just great. I like his stripy shirts, so down to earth. He truly respected women and understood our great movement of the twentieth century. A man of the people and so kind to all around him. A true artist."

Jack went last. When he said he liked Rousseau, they all started laughing and calling him a pleb.

"He paints post cards you fool, not

art," laughed Beatrice.

"He never left Paris, but painted jungles from his pleb cave on the outskirts of Paris," smirked Fiona.

"What a boring loser," yawned Tarquin.

"He's so ordinary beyond belief," joked St John, rolling his eyes and nearly falling off of his chair.

What Jack did not know was that all of these students had been to a special art appreciation summer school in Hampstead last year where they were told who are artists and who are not.

"and finally, there will be an artist of the year competition in four weeks' time. The Prince's art schools in London, Belfast, Glasgow, Cardiff and Leeds will be competing, so keep up your work, see you next week," and with that Professor Cringeworthy dismissed his class.

"My uncle knows the Prince and says he is such a bore," judged Fiona.

"Mind how you speak young lady, one day saying something like that will have a bad result for you," warned the Professor.

Jack had now gone within himself. He felt tired. He knew what he liked about Rousseau but didn't feel that he needed to justify his ideas and feelings to this crowd. The day had started to have an effect on him though. He had started to wonder how an ordinary boy like him could even begin to think of himself as an artist. He hadn't really thought about the idea of suburbia that much before. Maybe artists couldn't come from such a place and he started to doubt he really knew anything about how to think or what to be. He felt like giving up.

The students had now finished for the day. Jack started to hear the car horns sounding around four o'clock and knew what he would see when he left the art school. Sure enough as he walked through the exit door onto the street all the parent's cars were jostling for position. The Jaguar man had replaced his car with something much heavier, a Mercedes G Wagon and had attached the front with a steel wire from its winch to a lamp post. He would not now be moved by the Range Rover.

"Release the Wagon," shouted the excited father pointing to the lamp-post.

The children all got into their cars, the G-Wagon was unhitched and they all roared off in a blue fog of petrol fumes.

Chapter 5

Jack's mind was turning to what they would have for tea and what the featured matches on 'Match of the Day' would be. Jack was feeling quite thirsty as he walked along the pavement towards the tube station. It was a sunny late afternoon and he saw something glint on the pavement. It was a new fifty pence piece. Britannia gleamed upward, catching Jack's eye. He picked it up continued his walk. On the corner Jack could see a strange fresh juice stall, which wasn't there that morning on his way in to the art school.

Jack could hear something.

"Snnnnnort, snnnnnort, hisssss, hisssss, buzzzzzzzz, chitta chitta, oh-oo uhoo, sicsic sicsic."

He could make out the sounds of exotic and jungle animals coming from the stall. From the sound of macaws, toucans, monkeys and cicadas Jack felt he was going to see them at any moment. A smartly dressed man wearing a small bow-tie, oiled hair and a waxed moustache was serving the drinks to customers. Jack thought he looked familiar to him, in some way. Was he a football referee? He wasn't sure.

"I recommend the exotic fruit cocktail young sir," offered the smartly dressed man.

"It's a pound," said Jack pointing to the sign leaning against the stall, "I can't afford it."

"Look in your hand, what do you have?" smiled the smartly dressed man. And there, there in his hand were two fifty pence coins, new and shiny coins in his hand, right there. Jack was astonished.

"I'll have one then please."

Jack spent his pound on the drink and continued his walk to the station. It was now a warm early evening. As Jack entered the station, he showed his ticket to the woman in the ticket booth.

"Hello son," said the ticket collector, "that looks a nice drink, what's in it?"

"I think it's got mangoes in it and

pineapple, probably."

"Lovely. You had a busy day, you've got paint or something on your hands?" spotted the ticket office lady.

"Yes painting, very busy, I'm a bit tired really."

"You will be a great artist one day. I knows a thing or two about character. I can see it in your eyes. Character and artists. It's my thing," smiled the ticket lady with a nod of her head.

Jacked said his goodbyes and as he began to walk down the metal tipped stairs to the underground tube trains it seemed to get very warm. A young man, looking wild eyed and like a creature possessed ran past him, from the platform below.

Jack turned onto the northbound platform. He noticed that there was not a soul on the platform. He was quite alone, which was strange for that time of day. He felt a warm wind gently touching his face. He then saw the light of the train coming from the left and got ready to board.

The doors swished open and he got on. Again there was no one present, the carriage was completely empty. The doors closed and the train moved off, the familiar whine of the electric motors as they wound up, was replaced by the clickity-clack, clickity-clack of the steel wheels as the passed over the track joins. Jack closed his eyes and the clickity-clack, clickity-clack of the steel wheels started to be replaced by something else. He must be asleep and dreaming. The call of a macaw and the echo of baboon grunt wafted into the carriage.

Jack opened his eyes as the train

pulled into what should have been Hyde Park Corner. But it wasn't Hyde Park Corner. As the doors opened the smell and heat of the jungle entered the train carriage.

Suddenly the carriage was lit up by a flash of lightning and thunder shock the air like canon fire. The hot rain of a tropical storm blew inside and whipped Jack on his face. Then he heard a whine of a large wild beast, a whine and a shaking fear echoing through the jungle. The trees rose, running high up from the lush floor. Then Jack saw it, a flash of yellow and black stripe and that eye. IT WAS THAT EYE! The tiger's fearful eye formed a petrified stare. The fear seemed to be shining from the very soul of the beast. Its jaws were clenched showing distorted, chattering teeth. This was quite a site for a boy expecting to see the familiar surroundings of Hyde Park tube station. The clammy smell of a heated and wet jungle filled Jack's nostrils.

The rain came down in sheets upon the tiger, it tried to roar, but its deep, deep voice cracked with fear tightened vocal cords.

"The hunters have me, Giagia, at last, I am trapped in the teeth of steel and iron," gasped the tiger.

Jack had stepped from the train carriage and was now getting wet, while trying to shelter under the large leaves of a philodendron. He could feel the water down the back of his neck. He decided to move. The tiger bristled as he came closer.

"See here Giagia, Giagia wasn't it? I wish you no harm, I can help free you," offered Jack.

And, with a tug and a twist Jack released the tiger. He was holding something in his hand.

"Your paw was jammed and wedged into a strong tree root on the jungle floor," explained Jack with a genuine care and concern.

As Giagia moved Jack could see what looked like a piece of folded paper, released from the tiger's paw on the floor of the jungle. For as long as Jack could remember he had a passion for maps of all kinds, with his favourite being the tube map for the London Underground. He unfolded the paper to find a map, of a special kind. One side of the map was printed a message.

'For whoever should come in to possession of this map you must follow the one path of true glory, to find Love.'

The map almost seemed to be alive in Jack's hands, as he looked at it for clues for his journey. His position with the tiger, by what looked like an entrance was marked with a small drawing of Jack and the tiger, both of whom were walking in the direction indicated on the map.

Jack shook some of the rain from his

hair, smoothed it down and looked at the map, "Tiger, I shall follow this path and would welcome your company, if you'd like to come along."

"I will accompany my saviour, on his journey," offered the tiger with a sense of duty.

Jack could see that he needed to follow the path on the map, from the dark jungle to a small clearing where stillness and moonlight entered the jungle. As the jungle grew darker Jack could see the bright eyes of wild animals flashing in the heated undergrowth, where the baked and damp floor issued forth with steam and mist into the now chilling air.

The tiger and Jack walked for an hour before eventually coming to the clearing. The two figures on the map could now be seen arriving to the second marked point on the map.

As Jack was about to enter the clearing he stopped. He had seen something on the map, something moved, he was sure of it.

"What's that? What would David Attenborough do?" thought Jack to himself.

It was something moving towards its prey, it was a beast readying to strike a human.

"What is moving here tiger?"

He showed the map to Giagia and asked the tiger what he had seen.

"That is Basakeria, the killer lion of our jungle; he abides not by the code and takes the vulnerable and cherished at his will, sometimes for sport just to show his ugly power."

Jack felt the referee's football whistle in his jeans pocket, it was the really loud one for official matches that he had found left in the changing rooms at Ashton FC and asked Mr Murray if he could keep it when no one claimed it at the end of the season.

Jack reached into his Gola bag and retrieved the red acrylic paint from a tin. He made his face up like a wild angry beast and said to Giagia, "Come tiger we shall rush and scare the lion from its quarry tonight."

The tiger warned, "Basakeria will not be lightly denied his evening meal, think carefully Jack."

The pair went forward. They could now see that the human figure was in fact a sleeping minstrel. She was quiet and still as she slept in the moonlight. Jack could see her mandolin and water vase, close by her side. The moonlight was casting a cool shadow from the lion upon the cold sand.

The lion appeared to be using its nostrils to follow the scent of the minstrel, even though its eyes could have shown exactly where the woman lay.

Jack rushed forward, face aflame in painted red, with the Football Association Fox 40 Pearl whistle blowing out a hundred and forty decibels of crowd suppressing sound. Giagia ran by his side roaring a tiger roar.

Basakeria the lion confused and scared found himself a mile from the scene before he had time to even realise what had happened. His stomach was empty and hollow. He must eat and soon.

"Thank you young sir and to the fearsome beast. Please sit with me awhile," asked the Minstrel, catching her breath. Jack and the tiger nodded and sat down.

With a warm smile she laughed, "You have shown compassion to a poor minstrel, a stranger to you in this land"

They sat and talked with her a while.

She was kind and reminded Jack of the woman in the ticket office in Knightsbridge tube station.

"I am an artist on a journey," Jack found himself telling her. She looked thoughtful for a moment.

"I see," she nodded, "take some waters from my vase and pour into this small jar. For whenever you use this water to mix your paints you shall always paint with compassion."

They could hear the lion, Basakeria, roaring with anger and hunger in the distant hills.

"We need to remember the hurt we have caused to Basakeria, he will not look kindly upon us," and with that the tiger checked its claws, "we need to remember that such anger from one so powerful needs to find a balance in the jungle."

The Minstrel played them a beautiful song, a song of understanding, a song of finding compassion when on one's journey. The rhythms and scales were new to Jack's ear, different and mesmerising. The melody was simple and repeated again and again, in a weaving that pulsed through the cool evening air. The words of the song haunted Jack as he heard them.

Find me here by sandy banks
I shall remember this moment
With gratitude and thanks
The silence, the twilight peace
Your faces in the evening light
The richest treasure I shall carry
This memory between my hands.

This will be enough for me
As I fashion the Dragons Head

In this time of false idols and
Away with sadness and bitterness
Our mourning is soon at an end
Our yearning is soon at an end
Years past now in the wilderness

She stands as she ever has stood
Immovably founded in Grace
The hollow silence is there for those
Who turn inward on themselves?
We walk in circles not sensing loss
Living scenes from another's soul
Rich epiphany an elegant release
In our palace are angels and devils
No longer wondering day by day

In this time of false idols and

Away with sadness and bitterness

Our mourning is soon at an end

Our mourning is soon at an end

Years past now in the wilderness

Moments in truths of revelation

Making a dragon's head, an angel

A devil or perhaps a saint out of

stone

Finding wisdom beyond knowledge

Redemption from a love unknown

Forgotten Cassii have trod our

paths

When raised by the life-giving word

Sipping sweetness in communion

Comfort in the love of strangers

When she had finished her song, she withdrew something from her pocket.

"Before you go, take this phial with you. It contains the juice of a special leaf, which can calm all pain. Use it wisely Jack, for you shall need it," instructed the Minstrel

Jack packed the phial of concentrated erythroxylum leaf extract carefully into his Gola bag. Jack looked at his map. He could see himself and the tiger by the edge of the clearing. At the bottom of the map a small shield shape had appeared. On the shape was the word 'compassion' carved into the surface. Jack puzzled for a moment, in thought. They said goodbye to the Minstrel and pressed on into the night. Jack could see that on the map their next destination would be by a lake.

The moon lit their path as they walked

on out of the clearing and onto the next phase of their journey. After an hour, weary from effort the pair sat down on a dry and bare section of earth, next to a large mahogany tree that had come down in the storm.

Jack remembered that he had some Princes salmon paste sandwiches in his bag, a Harvest apple pie and a bottle of Tizer. He offered the tiger one of the sandwiches, which the tiger swallowed whole, in one, *guloup*!

Jack finished his meal and went to sleep listening to the heartbeat of the tiger. Jack was awoken by the call of a macaw, perched on the fallen tree. For a moment he knew not where he was. Jack then became aware of the macaw. He could swear that it was laughing in a high pitched gurgle. The macaw then sang a verse;

"She is simply splendid,
and no mistake,
she will bake you in a cake,
from Queen Fiona there is no escape,
you will be dead before the lake."

The macaw sounded a lot like Tarquin's mother from the art class. The macaw started to sing its verse once more;

"She is simply splendid,
and no mist......," sang the macaw.

The macaw had stopped as the tiger had opened one of its fearsome eyes and fixed it on the bird. The macaw flew into the canopy of the jungle with a few feathers dropping in fright.

"Who is Queen Fiona?" Jack asked

Giagia.

"For she is a tyrannical queen in this special jungle Jack. She is violent, fearful and weak, but commands the people with an elite force of assassins called the Commentatoris. They try and control what the people think and say. and if you do not comply with their wished they come for you, usually at dawn," said the tiger.

Jack looked at his map. He could see him and the tiger poised before the next marker on the map, five hundred yards further ahead on the path. The word Commentatoris had appeared on the map at the next marked point and the word appeared to be flashing.

Jack told the tiger and it said, "The macaws are her messengers, the bird will have told Fiona of our location and she will have dispatched her assassins. Be on your guard Jack, Fiona is jealous of you, of what you could be. You threaten her power. The Commentatoris are known to be so quiet, that their victims never hear their approach. Their horses wear velvet horseshoes and seem to glide over the jungle floor."

Jack and the tiger walked forward, looking into the jungle as they went until they reached the marked spot for the assassins to attack. Jack and the tiger kept their voices to a whisper, in the hush of the undergrowth. They could see nothing at all in the early morning light of day.

Jack noticed the leaves of large green succulent plants, they reminded him of the plants Nan had on the window sill at home. They were covered in droplets of dew from the chill of the night. Suddenly without warning, Jack felt a sharp pain in his side.

"Ah, ah," shouted Jack as he clutched his side.

He looked up to see the assassin's lance rise into the air for a second attempt on his life. The tiger sprang from under the large succulent leaves and swatted the queen's assassin from his horse. The tiger pinned the white robbed man to the floor with his left paw and raised his clawed right paw to slash the assassin's throat.

"Giagia, stop," said Jack, "let me

speak to my would-be killer."

The tiger paused and withdrew his mighty claws.

"Tell me who are you and what business do you have with me," demanded Jack, addressing the white robbed assassin.

"I am St John of the jungle and you 'my friend' are the outrider of the Sordidum, the one they call Jack, the plebe Jack. And now outrider of the Sordidum you shall die," laughed St John of the jungle.

And with that exclamation the assassin drew a curved dagger from his robe and lunged at Jack's heart. The tiger slammed the full weight of his clawed paw onto the forearm of the assassin and with his other paw threw the Commentatori against a tree rendering him unconscious.

A second assassin burst through the

jungle edge onto the path and galloped towards them, with his lance aimed at the back of the tiger, who had not seen or heard his arrival. Jack grabbed a fallen branch from the floor and as the lance was spearing into the side of the tiger Jack's heavy parry knocked the weapon to the ground. The assassin's horse reared up and threw the rider into the stump of an old mahogany tree, breaking his neck. Some moments later the tiger emerged from the jungle carrying the leaves of the Yarrow plant in his mouth.

"Place these leaves on your wound Jack and the blood will cease," said the tiger.

Jack made a poultice from the leaves and held it in place by tying his Leyton Orient scarf around it, under his shirt. He took a sip from the phial the Minstrel had given him and sat a while on the tree stump. Jack looked at the map. The word 'Courage' had joined Compassion onto the shield at the bottom of the map. Jack could still see the waning moon in the sky as he rose from the tree stump and stepped forward. Jack may have slept he was not sure.

The tiger asked, "Jack, you have lost blood, are you strong enough to continue?"

"Yes Giagia, I feel fine now, we have a journey to complete come on I want to move on!" pointed Jack towards the path.

The tiger got up and paced behind Jack as he continued his journey into the brightening morning. Two hours passed. The tiger, now leading stood still. Giagia had heard something. Jack paused he heard something too. A song drifted across the jungle. An insistent tune defined by a rhythmic pipe that almost sounded like an animal breathing. Jack stood motionless as he found himself drawn to the mesmerising sound, like a swirling wind of breath and enticement the tune continued. The tiger seemed similarly drawn and had a glazed shine in his fearful eye. The music sounded as if it were a conversation between distant voices, borne on the wings of birds of paradise. They drew closer to the, sound. Jack wasn't sure that he could feel his feet on the ground anymore; they seemed to have a life of their own.

A large water droplet fell from a leaf high in the canopy and landed on Jack's cheek.

"Glee-gloop, glee-gloop," little voices chanted.

He looked up and saw to his surprise

twenty sets of friendly eyes looking at him. He could see the green lime bodies, red eyes and orange legs of the jungle's tree frogs and they were singing him a simple song.

"You cannot go around the lake,
You cannot go over the lake,
You must go through the lake,
Without getting wet, without getting
wet"

Jack and the tiger came to an opening in the jungle, by the edge of a great lake. There they could see the Snake Charmer, back lit from the early sun and the reflected light from the lake.

"What's that moving?" asked Jack.

"Wait for the light and you will see Jack," mused the tiger with a slight shiver.

The jungle around the Snake Charmer seemed to move and shimmer and as Jack's eyes adjusted to the light he could see that black snakes hung from the trees and bushes and writhed on the floor in a mesmerised state. The pipes breathed and the snakes danced.

A shrill voice broke through the warm sound. Jack and the tiger could see a Roseate Spoonbill standing before the Snake Charmer.

"I am Beatrice and you shall do as I command. My feathers are dry and lustrous and precious to us all. Let me across the waters Snake Charmer and I will not spoon out your eyes," said Beatrice.

The snakes looked hungrily at the self-obsessed bird.

Jack heard the Snake Charmer say,

"To one so polite with distances to travel, answer me this for the crossing of the waters. Name me a six letter word that has I in the middle, in the beginning and at the end?"

The Roseate Spoonbill became very angry. She was not used to doing the bidding of others. She expected others to do her bidding!

"What, what, what nonsense is this!"

Beatrice, the angry Roseate Spoonbill, hopped onto a branch and made her way along it to carry out her threat of removing the Snake Charmers eyes with her spoonbill. In an instant a large black snake had struck the bird and had her in its powerful jaws. The snake intended to swallow her whole.

"*Help* me now," gasped the panicked Roseate Spoonbill called Beatrice.

"Now you say my name, for my name is Help and all you needed to do was use it." and with that the bird disappeared into the throat and stomach of the black snake. Jack could hear the bird's voice fading into the distance, "Help me now, help me now, help me now.............."

Jack and the tiger approached the Snake Charmer.

"I need Help", asked Jack politely, "and I know you are Help".

"A wise child. What do you wish for child?" asked Help.

Jack looked at the tiger and then found himself saying, "I wish to go further into the special jungle, to the expanse where all things are possible."

Jack wasn't sure where these words had come from, but they were his words, he had heard himself say them!

"You are looking for Hope I see, but you may have found something else as well," said the Snake Charmer, mysteriously.

"Tell me what you see slithering on the trees and across my shoulders?" asked the Snake Charmer.

Jack looked at the snakes and it reminded him of a painting that hung in his Nan's kitchen. Whenever Jack asked after the painting his Nan's only response was to say, "This is beauty".

Jack found himself automatically saying, "Beauty, this is beauty".

The Snake Charmer gasped and played a different happy tune, not mournful, but powerful upbeat and HAPPY. A song of celebration, for a rare and wonderful moment as the Snake Charmer had never heard the right answer before. Pap, pap pap, paaar-parp, it went, loudly with a rising and falling rhythm. When she had finished the Snake Charmer was full of praise, "Yes Jack, you have seen beauty and in places where none has seen it before."

The tiger, quiet through this time,

made itself close to Jack's side.

"I am Help, answer me this, said the Snake Charmer, "Name me a six letter word that has l in the middle, in the beginning and at the end?"

Jack heard the question and for some reason started to think of a photograph that his Nan kept wedged into the corner of the 'beauty painting'. It was a photograph of his mother and father pointing toward the distant horizon. His Nan used to say they were pointing Inland.

Jack without thinking said "Inland".

"Yes, correct Jack! L in the middle, IN at the beginning and at the end," smiled the Snake Charmer.

"I believe in you Jack. You are good through and through. But sometimes Jack beauty needs to be protected from HATE. I give you this glass phial. It contains the concentrated venom of six black mambas. This must only be used protect beauty against hate. It is a terrible position and one I do not give you lightly. Trust yourself on your journey and the true path will be yours," offered the Snake Charmer.

With that guidance the Snake Charmer started to play a different tune on the pipes and the water of the lake made a rushing sound, SHSHSHSHSHSHand a small narrow path parted for Jack and the tiger to pass along. Jack was amazed at the power of the Snake Charmer and was mesmerised by the walls of water rising on both sides. He could see fish looking at him as he walked.

After they had steeped along the dry path for an hour, they emerged back into the jungle. They rested for a moment. Jack studied the map and noticed the word BEAUTY, had appeared on his map. The tiger and Jack then came to a part of the jungle where there was thick succulent grass, heavy ferns and the sun shone yellow through the oversized hornbeams.

The silence was shattered by a scream, from a frightened animal. Directly in their path Jack saw Basakeria sink his fangs into the haunches of a startled antelope. It was in pain. The hungry lion had found its dinner. Jack could not stand the scream of the antelope. He fumbled for his Foxes whistle, with the intention of repeating his previously successful tactic in scaring off the lion.

Jack made ready to rush forward. Giagia placed his huge paw on Jack's shoulder and said, "What do you see Jack, do you see a horror?"

"Yes, it is horrible Giagia, a horror. I must stop it, let me go."

"Listen a moment, wait. The lion is showing the ZEST for life, can't you smell it Jack? The zest for life is the truth, how things are, what they are meant to be," said the tiger, "this is not sport now."

"I don't understand," said Jack, "the zest for life is dangerous."

Jack remembered when his Nan would explain to him why he did not have a Mum and Dad anymore.

She would say, "They had a zest for life Jack, a zest for the truth, which could not have been denied them. But now they are lost!"

The tiger untied his red neckerchief and walked slowly towards the lion, making sure that he could be clearly seen by the hungry lion. Basakeria paused as he saw the tiger approach. Giagia stood before him.

"Basakeria, we mean you no harm and will not deprive you of your rightful dinner. Let me mop your brow to show our respect for you in your successful kill," said Giagia in homage.

"You may mop my brow, but the boy stays there, where I can see him. He will die and be my breakfast if it is treachery that you mean," snarled Basakeria.

The tiger took his red neckerchief and mopped the radiating heat from the lion's hot and brow. The neckerchief became infused with the heat of the lion containing the ZEST for life. Jack stood back and was very still, whilst the tiger carried out his task. Jack began to feel and then understand the full depth of what he had seen. The law of the jungle had to him seemed cruel and random, but the lion was being a lion and the antelope an antelope. This was the TRUTH of this world, how it worked and what its nature was. To try and deny it would be futile and self-indulgent he thought.

As the tiger returned towards him Jack asked, "Is this the TRUTH, the TRUTH of the jungle Giagia?"

"Why yes Jack, this is the old and natural truth, learn it well and you will be on the path to wisdom," advised the tiger.

The tiger and Jack continued on their journey and they reached a less dense and more open section of the jungle. The sky was light blue and a light wind rustled the palm like leaves overhead. Jack sat for a moment on a large granite boulder and looked at his map.

There, on the shield at the bottom of the map, a fourth word appeared the word TRUTH.

After a further twenty minutes Jack and the tiger began to hear a murmur of human voices. They heard a variety of voices tut-tutting, a series of mocking laughs and cynical scoffing.

"Hah, hah, hah, oh, oh tut, tut, that won't do."

"How trite, what sugary tunes he wrote, not a decent melody amongst the work, no concept of atonal drama, a total absence of syncopation, devoid of dissonance" were the comments the tiger and Jack could hear as they approached the crowd.

A sign, fixed into well cut grass boarded by formal iron edging, stated that they were entering 'The Garden of Critics'. Jack could see well dressed pedestrians circling and pointing at a statue, moaning to each other about how bad that man was.

As he grew closer Jack saw that the pedestrians were walking clockwise around and around the statue. Jack and the tiger stood and looked up at the statue on the pedestal. Nan had kept an old 78rpm record at the back of the Dansette record cabinet, it was his Dad's record by Chopin; it was the 'Heroic' Polonaise in A flat major. Jack recognised it was this composer, his father's favourite, which was being ridiculed and criticised by the pedestrians. The critics reminded him of his classmates at the art school, he wasn't sure why.

A green parakeet landed on the statue. Three well dressed gentlemen picked up flint stones and threw them at the bird, making the bird squawk. Jack started to walk around the statue in an anti-clockwise direction. The critics suddenly gave him their full attention, as if they had just seen him for the first time. Like his classmates reaction to him in art school. The pedestrian critics started to point at him.

Someone shouted, "Teach him a lesson, what an uncouth yobbo he is."

As Jack continued to walk anti-clockwise all of the critics he passed started to bump into him. The more aggressive and vicious among them beat him with their parasols and walking sticks. Jack raised his arms to protect his head from a severe bruising. The walking sticks started to really hurt.

With his head throbbing Jack remembered a quote that his father had stuck in a scrap book, from long ago and sometimes used to read out loud:

*"In peace there's nothing so becomes a man as modest stillness and humility; but when the blast of war blows in our ears, then imitate the action of the **tiger**; **stiffen the sinews**, summon up the blood, disguise fair nature with hard-favoured rage."*

Jack smiled at remembering the quote. He then started to sing an old song he had learnt from his Nan. He wasn't sure why he started to sing it but he did. With a roar, he sang;

*"Now the moon shines bright on
Charlie Chaplin*

*His shoes are cracking, for want of
blacking*

*and his baggy khaki trousers still
need patching*

*Before they send him to the
Dardanelles."*

Jack walked forward into the onslaught of the critics and as their blows continued he felt nothing, only sadness at their waste of energy.

The tiger let Jack forge his own path, but then joined him in walking anti-clockwise against the crowd. The critics hearing Jack's voice and the voice and sight of the tiger, roaring the crowd cowered in their path and seemed confused. The conforming critics had failed to bully Jack. He had won his own path.

"I like the sound of Charlie Chaplin," commented the tiger.

"He's ok but we all liked Laurel and Hardy much better in my family."
Jack and the tiger completed their full circuit of the statue at their own pace, the tiger even tried to sing Jack's song as he was so happy. The tiger sang well in a deep baritone. Jack saw the word FORTITUDE had appeared on his map.

The jungle changed once again and the trees reminded Jack of an orchard he had seen in Sussex, rather than high trees of the jungle. It felt cooler as well, with the movement of air blowing throw the leaves in a pleasant way.

Jack then heard a whistle that sounded

familiar, was that a football whistle?

Jack heard someone shout, "On me head old chap, on me head when I run into the box."

"" 'ack im down Trev, don't let him through," shouted another as yet unseen voice.

And then there they were. Jack could not believe his eyes. There were a group of oddly dressed footballers training in the jungle. Some wore what looked like old fashioned blue and white striped bathing costumes and others wore the same garment but with yellow and red stripes. They had a brown leather football which they were now passing to each other over level ground.

As Jack and the tiger stood on the edge of what was the pitch the stripy jerseys rushed by. Jack could see that this group of footballers were training for a big match. The training changed to a five a side practice match.

Jack and the tiger watched the match for a few minutes. Jack then shouted, "Can I come on as a sub," to the player who seemed like the captain and looked like his Art

Teacher.

"Of course Jack, on you come, I thought you'd never ask," said the football captain.

Jack ran onto the pitch and joined in. After a few minutes he scored a brilliant goal. He started organising the players, getting them to create new moves on and off the ball. After thirty minutes and four more goals the training session finished. The front three players moved and understood Jack, just like his three friends Dan, Steve and Ben.

"We have a big match this afternoon against the jungle champions, The Monkeys, we want you to be our mid-field dynamo, will you do it?" asked the captain, who was like Mr Burns the Art Teacher.

"Of course," answered Jack, his side

wound now seeming almost entirely healed.

The footballers and the tiger had a light lunch of tinned salmon and cucumber sandwiches sitting on striped patterned deckchairs. Just after lunch Jack could hear the sound of pounding drums as The Monkeys and their entourage of marmosets, lima sand baboons arrived. They strutted around in a happy and positive spectacle. Singing and beating their chests.

"HEAR the MAGIC, boom boom boom, SEE the MAGIC boom boom boom, FEAR the MAGIC boom boom boom, FOOTBALL MAGIC boom boom boom"

The jungle champions set up trestle tables and unpacked their food and had their lunch as well. The captain came over and he shared a cup of tea with the stripy captain.

A Toucan, wearing a referee's

uniform, sat himself on the main table in the middle of the pitch. The Toucan called to the two captains, "Over here boys please, at the double."

Jack thought the Toucan sounded just like Mr Murray, if Mr Murray was somehow transformed into a speaking bird.

"We've heard you've got a new player called Jack, is that right?" asked the Monkey's captain.

The Toucan referee looked at the stripy team captain with a question in his eyes, "Yes, Jack is new, but he has been known about and registered for some time. We knew he was coming and now he is with us," said the stripy team captain.

"That's ok then," instructed the Toucan, "I want a clean game of football. The rules of the jungle do not apply to the field of play for either team. I see you have those two trouble makers still in your team captain, Formaldehyde and Crispin. Make sure they behave young sir and let's play football," said the Toucan with a stern look. Both captains nodded their agreement.

"But boys, before we start, join me in the jungle football anthem," called the Toucan, "all stand to attention!"

The Toucan then sang an extra-ordinary football song, waving to the crowd to join in;

You've come play the lovely football
The beautiful game of football
Just put on your kit 'n' tie up your boots
It's just the lovely football
Dial the number give 'n' us a call
Clap your hands when that one like

Keegan shoots

Make that tackle, slot that pass
I'm right at home when I'm on the grass
We're playing with a back line three
Use the flying full backs and cross to me
When the crowd begins its chants
You simply forget all your can't 's'
Feel your heart soar!

Keep the ball right on the floor
Right on the floor.

Trust in the beautiful game
Keep on practising and you'll find fame
Just put on your kit 'n' tie up your boots
It's just the lovely football
Dial the number give us a call
Clap your hands when Keegan shoots

Make that tackle, slot that pass
I'm right at home when I'm on the grass

We're playing with a back line three

Use the flying full backs and cross to me

When the crowd begins its chants

You simply forget all your can't 's'

Feel your heart soar!

Keep the ball right on the floor

Right on the floor.

When the singing had finished Jack took up his position in the mid-field. He had borrowed a pair of football boots but was still wearing his jeans. The Toucan blew his whistle and the game began. Jack immediately had the ball and quickly learnt that The Monkeys had not seen anyone make a dummy move before. Jack kept selling dummies to the Monkeys giving him so much time on the ball it seemed as if he were playing without any opposition at all.

After a time Jack looped over a precise ball for his forward to volley into the net. It was a wonderful move. One of the Monkeys was becoming increasingly annoyed with Jack's ability. The tiger could see this from the touch line.

The tiger sighed to a panda standing next to him, "I do hope the Monkeys behave, I remember what happened last year against the Chimps."

Jack received the ball from his defence and intended to wrap a curved ball to one of the wingers who he could see was making a run when two Monkeys ran into him at full pelt. Jack went down like a sack of potatoes. The Toucan blew his whistle for the foul.

The tiger remembered that, "This is the kind of cheating that won it for the Monkeys last

year, the referee is under a lot of pressure."
Jack was dazed, but eventually regained his
composure.

The Monkeys captain was furious at
his two teammates and was shouting at them
through the noise of the large crowd of
animals that had gathered.

"We don't win like that do you
understand! I will not have it. The Chimps
still don't talk to me on the committee and
it's your fault!"

He finally finished, turned his back
and walked away from them. The stripy
team were awarded a free kick thirty yards
out from the Monkeys goal. Jack had been
asked to take the kick. Would he pass or
shoot, that was the question the crowd were
asking each other?

The tiger had moved away from the

Panda and was keeping a close eye on the two fouling Monkeys. He was sure they were still up to no good. and there it was. The two Monkeys had carefully chosen two stones to throw at Jack as he took his run up. The Monkeys arms moved back ready to unleash their missiles at Jack's head. They did not see the tiger make his way along a thick branch which extended over the pitch. Just as Jack started his run up the tiger swatted the two Monkeys with the back of his poor, knocking them over and allowing Jack to deliver a tremendous top-spun dipping free kick. Over the wall of the high jumping Monkeys it went and into the back of the net. The referee blew his whistles and brought the game to an end. Some of the Monkeys ran to the referee to complain about the tiger, but the Toucan would not hear any criticism of his decision to award the goal. The Monkeys' captain was extremely gracious and embarrassed about his two cheating players.

"I will never field Formaldehyde and Crispin again, they have brought shame to us," said the Monkeys captain to the gathered crowd. The captain sent Formaldehyde and Crispin home and were not allowed to join in the celebrations and party.

After the match the Monkeys wanted Jack to teach them about making dummy moves, so he did. The Monkeys started to try the dummy out for themselves.

Jack coached them that, "It's all in the eyes and in the upper body movement; you can send them any way you want with that."

They loved the move and held Jack aloft as if he were on their team. As they all trooped off the field for afternoon sandwiches and tea everyone was happy and full of JOY.

The Monkeys invited Jack and the tiger and the stripy team to a feast that very evening at their jungle home, which they all accepted. Jack sat in a deck chair and spoke to the tiger.

"I am grateful to you Giagia for keeping an eye out for me," thanked Jack, "those two didn't know how to play fair."

"That is true Jack, they could not play fair and will never know the wonder of joy which you brought to your game."

Jack withdrew his map from his pocket. He could see the sixth word JOY had appeared at the bottom of the page. He looked at it for a moment and then replaced it into his pocket. That night Jack, Giagia and the footballers, the referee, the Panda and a collection of the spectators of the match made their way to The Monkeys home.

Jack thought the music was fantastic. The drumming was catching a rhythm that was getting everyone dancing. There were huge bowls of fruit of all kinds which the Monkeys had gathered from the trees. Tables covered with plates of baked potatoes, roasted carrots and parsnips cooked in underground pits, were there for everyone to help themselves. It was a lovely time. Jack and the tiger ate their fill.

When the darkness came to the jungle, Jack, the tiger, the Monkeys and the footballers sat round a fire, to laugh and tell stories. It came time for the last story. The captain of the footballers stood up and told of a great man and woman that came into the jungle many years ago.

"Up to that time, we lived in fear and had no lives of our own. Queen Fiona controlled everything. If we showed the slightest sign of doing what we wanted she would send the ORTHODOX POLICE to force you to obey, or the Commentatoris to kill you," said the footballer's captain.

"How did they change things for the better for everyone?" asked Jack.

"They taught us to stand up for ourselves by just being who we were, no more and no less. They would paint huge murals with their spray cans showing us that we had nothing to fear," said the footballer's captain, "they needed to overcome the IN CROWD as well. They were the courtiers of Queen Fiona and competed to be the most loyal to her."

The Toucan said, "The lives of everyone got better when they arrived. They defeated ORTHODOX POLICE and the IN CROWD. There was a great battle of wit, creativity and mental strength at the annual Fiona's Fair. In every field the great man and women defeated Queen Fiona's champions. It didn't matter if it was poetry, singing, painting, dancing or debating the elegant couple succeeded in showing Fiona's hoards as fakes and imposters. That night a great gathered crowd of the people rebelled casting aside the shackles that the Queen had held them down with."

Jack felt an electric buzz in his head. He somehow knew as the story was being told that the couple were his mother and father.

"Where are the great man and woman now, do they live among you, are they here?" asked Jack.

The drumming ceased. All grew quiet. The head of the Monkeys eventually spoke up, "I will tell you Jack. Queen Fiona was defeated, many stayed loyal and even now in her current state she commands the Commentatoris. She packed up her belongings onto an old cart and prepared to leave the stone castle on the Augend Rocks. As she came out from under the portcullis a man in a long purple robe, over a red shirt with white collars stood in her way. The ex-Queen paused and demanded for the man to move to the side. He refused and pulled a black conductors baton from his pocket. As he did so he swirled the baton into a series of whirling sounds and rhythms. The Queen seemed to shiver, then sprouted whisker sand then became a striped cat.

The head of the Monkeys continued, "She had been captured by the jungle's most powerful being the smoking man, Captain Capstan non Filtre. He had once been one of the Queen's suitors, but she had rejected him years before. Once Captain Capstan non Filtre had taken the Queen's castle on the rocks he lured the great man and woman to his new home pretending that he was their friend, as he had defeated the evil Queen. A banquet was held, but, once the dinner was over the couple fell asleep, as they had been drugged by Captain Capstan non Filtre."

"But where are they, are they dead?" asked Jack.

"You see Captain Capstan non Filtre, captures his victims and slowly dries them out before making them into tobacco. It is a ten year drying process he says. The couple arrived here ten years ago tomorrow, so they may still be alive, but deep within the castle on the rocks. They will be very, very dry liked old tobacco."

"That's enough. Thank you. I'm off on my path. I know what it has to be."

Jack decided immediately to rescue his Mother and Father from the smoking Captain. Within thirty minutes Jack was on his way.

Jack looked at his map. Immediately it came to life. "Look Giagia, see what it is showing me?"

The ground started to get rocky. But

Jack used his map to take him to Capstan's jungle hideaway castle on the rocks using the best and easiest path.

"I see it, we must be careful" growled the tiger looking upward.

Jack could see it as well. The castle was built into a series of caves, into a steep slope. The tiger carried two large urns of water, strapped over his shoulders, to revive Jack's parents if they found them.

Two monkeys from the football team accompanied the tiger and Jack, swinging in the trees and then scampering over the rocks keeping a look-out on the way to the castle.

"Look at that," pointed Jack, looking vertically up.

After two hours they had come to a cliff face. The tiger and Jack began to climb to a cave opening, with the monkeys help.

They were all breathing very hard with the exertion of the climb.

"Come Giagia and Jack, keep low into the surface and you shall climb," sang the Monkeys.

It was hard going and the very steep and rough ground, but Jack had managed to borrow a pair of Gola all weather football boots from his stripy team mates, so that he had good grip up the slope.

Eventually and with little breath, they reached the entrance to the cave and the start of the castle complex. Queen Fiona as the striped Tabby Cat appeared.

"Oh, if it isn't that loser Jack and his big fat cat, too much nosh and not enough dosh," laughed Fiona, who as part of the transformation from Queen to cat had been condemned to speak in rhyme.

"Where are my parents, Fiona? I must find them and save them," said Jack.

"When I sent my Commentatori, I expected them to be covered in glory, with your death all so gory, but you're here now so it's another story," rhymed Fiona.

"I will save them, out of my way," shouted Jack.

"You will not save them boy, they are dried out and will no longer annoy, the great smoking man who will defeat your plans, on your way before he makes you pay!" Fiona deliberately distracted Jack and the tiger enabling the smoking Captain to drop a large and strong net over both Jack and the tiger from the roof of the cave. She still hoped the Captain would change her back if she was nice and useful to him.

The smoking Captain said, "Ah Jack

and Giagia, I will leave you to dry here under net and in dry cave with summer's heat for five years, I shall then, …ahem, ahem."

At this point the smoking man had a large and sustained coughing fit. It went on, cough, cough, cough and on. The smoking man's eyes had become full of tears with the effort of coughing. It was a really serious cough. Jack has an idea.

"Listen Captain you should stop smoking, its making that cough of yours very bad, I can hear it, can't you hear it Giagia?" asked Jack.

"Why yes Jack, this is a most serious cough and one that must have relief from smoke," replied the tiger.

"You know nothing Jack. Anyone knows that smoking is good for you, it clears your lungs out and gives you something to do with your hands when you are thinking and I think a lot," said the smoking Captain, with his best thinking face jutted out into the world.

"It's daft smoking. Makes you ill and you will die," said Jack.

"Nonsense, all the big Hollywood Stars smoke, like John Wayne, Steve McQueen, all of them," said the smoking Captain, "I've collected their cards from the packets."

"They both died of smoking Captain, you obviously don't read the papers," said Jack truthfully.

"I don't need facts! I am the Captain!" At that moment the Captain had another coughing fit.

"I have such a dry sore throat,

though" said the Captain.

"I have just the thing for you Captain, it is the best medicine for throats that you will ever have, I will prepare it for you," persuaded Jack, "come along, listen to my friend sing."

The tiger began a slow and smoky sounding blue song, which made the smoking Captain feel mellow and he nodded his approval of Jack's medicine idea.

Giagia smiled at Capstan and sang:

You were livin' in a state of grace
But you started smokin' 'n' ined
your face
Your soul shifted to somewhere
unknown
and your weakness to your family
shown

You're living in sin

But think you are living in Salvation

You're living in sin

Your soul's sinking in desolation

Seeking salvation I say to you

The sins of the fathers will make you

blue

You think that everything you do is

right

But smokin's a sin with us here

tonight

You're living in sin

But think you are living in Salvation

You're living in sin

Your soul's sinking in desolation

163

Guilt is a stone, it's heavy, to carry
But a fool's ego's you cannot bury
When ya' love smokin, everythin'
stinks
Never mind what ya' lovin' family
thinks

You're living in sin
But think you are living in Salvation
You're living in sin
Your soul's abomination of
desolation

You think that you can't do anything
wrong
Smokin' on tha' cigarette 'ya feel so
strong
But get a grip and make a righteous
choice

Be true to yourself and hear his
voice

Whilst the smoking Captained watched the tiger, Jack with great VISION got out his erythroxylum leaf liquid in the glass phial, that he had received from the Minstrel. The Captain was feeling relaxed hearing the tiger's voice and his throat was still very sore. When the song finished Jack gave the phial to the smoking Captain. He slowly drank it, letting the liquid slowly pass his sore throat. His face began to widen into a smile as his throat started to feel much, much better.

"Oooooh that's nice."

"Now let me see the dry man and woman" says Jack to Capstan.

Jack knew that his mother and father would soon be dead, even if they were still alive now.

"My throat is feeling better already. No I will not show you, why should I, I am all better."

"I can give you an even more powerful phial if you show me, as what I have given you will only last for twenty four hours. My other medicine is a cure," bluffed Jack.

"Oh, alright, come with me," said Capstan, "that sounds like a good deal for me."

Jack, the tiger and Fiona were led to a dry and dusty space by the Captain.

"This is it. This is it. The long term drying room."

Jack saw his mother and father laid out on straw drying in the sun.

"There they are, they are almost dead

and done, my treat to the world, give me the phial," said Capstan.

"Don't drink it all at once, make it last, it's all I have" says Jack, knowing that the Capstan didn't have the willpower to delay the consumption. Jack had given the Capstan the phial from the Snake Charmer.

The Capstan just laughed as he downed the terrible mamba venom.
There was an immediate and not all together beneficial effect on the Captain. His face was the first indication that all was not well.

Fiona shrieked her cat shriek and said, "What have you done to my poor old suitor, he's gone all grey, the colour of pewter."

The Capstan convulsed through different colours and shapes, finally settling into a light grey. Fiona looked terrified at these events and ran away, her stripy coat disappearing deep into the castle caves.

Chapter 6

"I will help you Jack."

The tiger ripped his neckerchief into two and dropped a piece into each of the jugs containing water. The neckerchief contained the zest of life from Basakeria. Jack's parents were the colour of dried sand and were perfectly still. Any movement, from his parents and Jack was sure that they would break into millions of fragments. Jack carefully poured the water over his mother and father. The tiger shaded the two from the sun with its great body, casting a long shady shadow. The two monkeys fanned Jack's parents with large leaves.

After a few minutes both parents started to get their colour back. Jack could see his mother and father open their mouths, so he knelt down near them to hear what they would say. They opened their mouths but could not speak. Jack, not wishing to choke them, carefully poured the remaining water into their mouths.

"Giagia I think we are too late, they are gone and I shall never hear their voices again," cried Jack, his face showing a deep sadness.

"Remember Jack, the zest of life is very, very strong. Have faith in your parents and their strength. Their strength runs through your veins as well," encouraged Giagia.

The Monkeys fanned and the tiger shaded Jack's parents for an hour, until the heat of the sun started to fade from the cave and a coolness crept in from the jungle. A light mist drifted in the mouth of the cave and chilled everything it touched. Jack could feel his arms become cold and he almost felt himself shiver.

"Is this good, this cold, do you think?"

But then Jack noticed his mother move first. Her eyelids fluttered and then her eyes opened.

"Hello Mum," welcomed Jack kindly as he held her hand, "it's me Jack I'm here Mum."

"Have I been asleep Jack? I have been having an extraordinary dream that I was in a desert looking for water. Each oasis that I found turned out to be either dry or a mirage. I wasn't sure which was worse no water or no real oasis," rasped Jack's Mum, with a dry and faint voice.

She moved her arms and held Jack

tight around his neck and then kissed him.

"I love you Jack, how on earth did you find us?" asked Jack's Mum, "we have been gone so long now."

At that moment Jack's father began to stir. Jack then heard a song that he had almost forgotten, a song his father sang him when he was happiest with his battered guitar. It was an old sea shanty. His father began quietly at first, but then repeated loudly:

"We'll rant and we'll roar like true British sailors
We'll rant and we'll roar across the salt seas
Until we strike soundings in the Channel of Old England
From Hoy to Scilly is thirty-five

leagues

I'm fair parched like an 'ol piece a
paper

I'll drink an English stream 'f all its
waters"

"Hello Jack, me darlin'," smiled Jack's father, still keeping up the salty dog pretence, as he grabbed Jack and held his son him to him.

"Dad, you're back, what are you doing here in this place?" asked Jack.

Jack's father got up from the straw, walked over and kissed his wife, in silence. He drank some more water from jugs the Monkeys had found.

"Thank you," he nodded to the Monkeys.

"It's a long story Jack. You were so

young when we went away; I am guessing you don't know much about your Mum and me. We asked Nan in our dreams to keep a lot of it quiet as we wanted you to have a fair chance in life."

He looked across at Millie, Jack's mother and she sensed he was asking her permission. She nodded her ascent.

"Your mother and me met at art school, Waltham Forest College to be exact. It wasn't very well known at the time, being in the east end of London and was not fashionable like the Slade, Camberwell, St Martin's and the rest. I lived in Leytonstone and your Mum was from Chingford.

We had some great tutors at the college in the early '60s, including Peter Blake. I learnt a lot from him Jack. We had really good studios there, high ceilings, good light, lovely canteen where we all ate; the college had a famous catering course so all the students basically lived at the college. Anyway your mother and I both developed our different styles and we both dreamt of being artists and making our lives together as well. We didn't have any sponsors or rich parents to help us out. We needed to earn a living and to be doing something we believed in, to support ourselves and our art.

So we both became teachers and started work in Waltham Forest in the late '60s. I worked at McShane School and your mother worked at The Blue School, as they called it.

"Where did you live then? In Wood-ford?"

"No. We lived in Barratt Road Walthamstow, off of Wood Street and then we had you in 1968. We could walk to work from there. We converted our lean-to into a studio and we made our work. We both developed a graffiti art style. I was very abstract, ultra urban and modern, a bit sci-fi. Your mum painted back-drops for performance artists, very conceptual, some realistic others more distortions of time and space. We were modern.

We got quite well known in late sixties underground London. Nan used to babysit for us so we could go to different events or 'happenings' as they were sometimes called. One Friday night we got a call that there was a sort of art protest down on Fish Island, near Stratford. All the materials would be provided; all we had to do was turn up and do our thing. We got off the tube at Hackney Wick, after leaving you with Nan and walked over to Bream Street on the Island. They had a warehouse there open on one side, with boards, aerosols, paint everything we needed all set up on a stage at the front. There were guys on megaphones and the crowd was getting big. We were half way into our work, when we heard a roar go up and then some screams. As we were up high, on a sort of temporary stage we could see what was happening. A gang of men dressed in black, led by a man with blond hair and a leather jacket were laying into our crowd with pieces of pipe. I said to your Mum let's get out of here. We started running, back towards Hackney Wick Station, it was getting late by then, around eleven o'clock. As we jumped on the train going east, I thought I saw some figures in black jump on the carriage behind us. The train had graffiti art on it from a friend of ours called Jaundice. As the train started up a group of five of them burst through the carriage connecting door and came straight for us at the other end, they had bits of pipe and iron bars. Then I recognised, the blond man at the front of the gang, it was Brown. There's much more to tell about Brown and his wife. We got up and ran, opening the connecting doors and kept going. They caught us by the last door before the driver. It started to go a bit weird then, like one of your Mum's paintings. Time and space seemed to move about, with the metal bars just passing through us, as the gang leader with the leather jacket tried to give us a beating. We came to, in the jungle and have been here since," said Jacks father.

"We found out from our friend

Jaundice, who arrived a week after us, that the papers had said that we were laying graffiti onto a stationary tube train in a siding and that we got hit by a fast train smashed to smithereens as no bodies were found and that's why we had gone missing," said Jack's mother, "it made us sound like criminals."

Jack's mother and father were now sitting up and the colour had returned to their skin. Jack's mother held Jack close and spoke into his ear, smoothing his hair with her hand like she used to when he was little.

"Jack, Jack, it's so lovely to be with you I can hardly breathe! Your Dad and I put loads of our materials, sketch books, photographs and some pieces the week before this happened, in Nan's shed. She said she would look after it, store it, whilst we were looking for a new house, we were moving from Walthamstow," said Jack's mother.

"Nan's got it all locked up, she's got two locks on it. I've never been inside. I live with Nan, just us two. There is this eye painted high up on the wood."

"That's your Mums tag," nodded Jack's father, "the all seeing eye, kind of dramatic. She was known for it on all of her paintings."

The two monkeys had fetched some more water in the jugs and had found some food from the castle kitchen. The tiger awoke from his sleep on the cave floor and came and sat by Jack.

"I see you've made a friend in Giagia," said Jack's mother, "he has been our companion since we arrived here and helped us defeat the Orthodox Police. It's like being at home really, all different but all the same."

Jack had been waiting for his moment, he now said, "You are coming back to Woodford with me, aren't you, you must. Let's get ready, let's go."

Before Jack's parents could answer he heard the sound of a carnival rhythm, beating and getting closer and closer to the caves and castle.

Jack's mother and father then started singing a duet together, which sounded like an old show song from the 1950s.

They sang:

> *"Somewhere in the world*
> *There is morning*
> *Without warning*
> *In the morning*

Somewhere in the world

There is morning

and I want to spend

That morning with you

It could be in Plymouth Sound, how profound

Derbyshire or Frome

Livin' in a shiny caravan, in old Afghanistan

Timbuktu or Rome

Somewhere in the world

Is afternoon

With no gloom

In the afternoon

Somewhere in the world

Is afternoon

and I want to spend

That afternoon with you

It could be in Cardiff Bay tha' would
be gay
Essex or Kent
Driving in New York State, on a date
Lyon or Ghent

Somewhere in the world
It is evening
When we're old and grey
We've had a lovely day
Now we're old and grey
Somewhere in the world
It is evening
and I chose to spend
My life, with you

When they finished singing, Jacks mother and father looked at each other with a great love.

"This is a special time Jack. A carnival is coming to celebrate. You must listen and understand now. We know we cannot leave the jungle. We are here now Jack. The power, the force brought us here was for a purpose. There was a shift, a shift which took us away from death and into this jungle. There was a job to be done here, which we started and must now finish. It is not your time yet Jack. We love you and don't want to part again ever, but it is not your time, do you see?" sighed Jack's mother with great pity.

"We are in this world now Jack," Jack's father smiled a said smile.

Jack's mother and father hugged him

for what seemed an all too brief moment.

"You must return now to Woodford," says Jack's father, "to live, live your life to the full."

Jack cried great warm tears down his face. His mother gave him something wrapped in brown paper and he put it in his jacket inside pocket.

"Remember, we LOVE you Jack and we always will."

"You are as good as anyone Jack and you can do, be or achieve anything that you want to and don't let anyone make you feel that you don't belong or don't deserve. You deserve everything," waved Jack's father. They both then said, "Give our love to Nan".

"Beware, of the Browns," warned Jack's father over his shoulder, "beware, of the Browns," he repeated.

The carnival had arrived at the mouth of the cave, with the rhythm pounding out an incessant beat, boom, boom, ba, ba boom, drawing his mother and father away. Jack could see the Minstrel with her m mandolin in the crowd, strumming her strings in time with the beat. and there was the Snake Charmer, with the pipes sounding high and low notes simultaneously making the melody. When Jack turned back to look at his parents they were transformed and dressed as Columbine and Pierrot, as the carnival King and Queen.

"This is the night carnival Jack, we love you," shouted both Jack's parents.

The Minstrel filled with a powerful vision sang a song of both longing and fulfilment that bewitched all present with a sorrowful glee.

Jack's parents held hands and

followed the carnival down the rocky path away from the castle. Jack and the tiger followed. Jack knew that he was seeing his parents move away from him and the ache inside him hurt more and more, more than anything he had ever endured before. Jack hung his head but followed the carnival down, with the tiger by his side. When the party arrived at the base of the rocks Jack's parents were possessed by a leaving dance. His parents joined the dancing procession. The bodies we all silhouetted against the moonlit sky. They were dark figures that could be seen against the light from the moon.

Jack looked saw the faces of his mother and father for final time, their hands held as one, as they danced towards dawn and the dark jungle. Jack looked against the coming stormy sky. He held his face in his hands and rocked back and forth on his heels. He hoped the rain would wash away the tears from his face. He took his hands away from his face looked up and as the first thunder cracked and they were gone.

Jack watched as the procession head off and disappeared into the dark. Jack sobbed and cried, until he ached. He had not felt a sadness and pain as strong as this, ever. He found it unbearable, to think that he had been with his parents and now would not be with them.

Jack felt the tiger's paw, holding him on his shoulder. He sat down. The tiger purred, "Jack, look at your map and see your destination."

Jack looked at his map and he could see that a seventh word VISION had appeared, accompanied by LOVE at the final and eighth in large letters. Jack remained seated with the tiger for some time and he may have slept, he wasn't sure.

When he awoke he found himself resting on the tiger on a sandy pathway. He started walking with the tiger. Eventually they came to an open space. The trees were further apart and looked as if they had been planted in an orderly fashion, by a gardener.

"You remind me of someone I know," smiled Jack, to the tiger.

"Then I shall be always with you Jack and in your memory," said the tiger, "you have a destiny now, where you will realise who you really are. We must part now."

And with these words the tiger placed his paw once more on Jack's shoulder and nudged him forward with his nose, on his own. Jack hugged the tiger's neck and walked on. Jack could see a road. In the road was a horse and cart. The cart was black with orange wheels and the horse was a dappled grey with a blinkered harness. As Jack grew closer he realised that the driver was someone that he had seen before. It was the well dressed moustachioed man who had sold him the exotic fruit cocktail.

As Jack reached the horse and cart the moustachioed driver said,

"Room in the back for one, next stop the Central Line. I said won't that be fine, the Central Line, nice and red, get out of your bed."

"Thank you, sir."

The two little dogs barked, but seemed to smile at him. The wagged their tails to show that they were friendly.

"Hello madam, what lovely dogs you have."

Jack smiled at the small child in the cart and reached up to pat he dogs. He climbed up onto the cart using the cast iron foot step.

"Have you had a good trip Jack?" asked the moustachioed driver.

Jack's face was strained with the second loss of his parents. He had not been able to have time to deal with his feelings. He wasn't always very good at knowing what to do with how he felt.

"Thank you driver, it's a trip I will remember forever and treasure," replied Jack.

"Keep your map safe, young sir, keep it with you always," advised the moustachioed driver with a caring look to Jack.

Jack could hear the clip clop of the horse's hooves on the hardened road surface. The rhythm of the hooves and the sway of the cart rocked him to sleep. The rock and the rhythm, the rock and the rhythm, like a pendulum tapping out a calming sound.

Chapter 7

When he awoke he immediately felt cold. He shivered, and before he opened his eyes he could smell a familiar smell. There was mustiness in the air, a mix of tough upholstery, captured human atmosphere and Jeyes fluid. Before he opened his eyes Jack knew that he was on a Central Line tube carriage. The train was not moving. Jack looked out of the window, it was still light. Jack recognised that he was at Loughton Station, in one of the sidings. Jack banged on the driver's door, as he thought he could hear movement. The grey door open and the driver stood there with his bag and handle.

"In the land of nod were you, boy? Come on, come with me and I will get you onto the platform," helped the driver.

"Thank you," Jack gave the driver the thumbs up.

Jack felt very tired still and extremely thirsty like he had been in the desert. He thought that he must have fallen asleep on his way back from the art class, or was there something in the cocktail, he wasn't sure.

When they got to the platform Jack waved, "Goodbye, thanks for getting me here."
The driver acknowledged him with a doff of his cap through the driver's window. Jack caught the next westbound West Ruislip train to Woodford. His mind was in a whirl, but being very tired, he concentrated on not falling asleep again and just getting back home. Jack could see it was six thirty, so he was only thirty minutes later than normal.

"Hello Jack," said Nan when she

opened the front door, "I was beginning to get a bit worried about where you were. Everything alright?"

"Yes Nan, just a busy day over there," said Jack, meaning the art school.
Nan could see something had changed within Jack. She wondered what it was but had a sense that it was something significant.

"Seeing that we didn't have fish and chips last night I have made fish fingers and chips and peas tonight."

"Thanks Nan I am very hungry, can I have some bread as well?"

"Yes Jack, I got a nice crusty loaf from Ingels," said Nan.

Jack and his Nan sat down and had their fish fingers and chips for dinner, with a strong cup of tea. After dinner Jack could hardly keep his eyes open, but still watched a Match of the Day season highlights programme before falling asleep in the armchair. He woke with a jolt and went to bed. Nan knew something had happened to Jackand she waited for the next day to see what it was. The next morning Jack got up, had a bath and then got dressed. Before breakfast he wanted to go to the newsagent on the corner to get his 'Shoot' magazine, as he didn't have a chance to get it on Saturday. As he put his Jacket on he felt something in the pocket. He sat on the chair in his room and got it out.

It was his map. His map from the jungle. So it was true. He opened the map up. A new message had appeared on the map.

The message said,"You are a great, great painter Jack, look at your map and you can see that you have everything that you need – Compassion, Courage, Beauty, Truth, Fortitude, Joy, Vision and Love – you are a true artist Jack. The real deal, you just havent realised it, yet, but now you will!"

Jack could feel that there was something else in his jacket. He got it out. It was wrapped in brown paper. He unwrapped the packageand there it was the artist's paint brush that his mother had given him in the castle cave. Jack was astounded. As Jack held the brush he knew that he could paint anything. **Anything!** No matter what subject, what idea, what style, what reality, with this brush it could be accomplished. He just felt and knew he could paint anything.

Jack went downstairs. Nan was waiting for him at the kitchen table with the yellow formica top.

"What is it Jack, what happened yesterday?" asked Nan.

Jack went through the whole story starting with the exotic coacktail and then the journey and destinations through the jungle. When Jack got to the bit about his mother and father Nan's eyes welled up. Jack showed his Nan the brush and the map. Nan said she recognised the hand writing, it was her daughter's, Jack's mother.

She held Jack's hand tight and said, "Jack, I've always tried to protect you from what happened to your Mum and Dad. When they disappeared people wrote lots of horrible and nasty things about them in the papers. They said they were anarchists out to ruin our countryand sort of said it was their fault that they had been hit by a train and disappeared. I never believed it of course.

But I wanted to shield you from it, so you could learn about it when you were older. They speak to me in my dreamsand I listen."

" I know, they told me."
Nan nodded a thoughtful look.

"Is that why the shed is all locked up? Dad told me they were in the middle of moving from Walthamstow when they ended up in the jungleand had stored their art stuff in your shed."

"That's right, its all in there Jack, half finished works, paints, brushes all their materials that they didn'y want to risk losing in the move," said Nan.

Nan went to her room and brought out two keys and a can of WD40.

"Come on Jack, lets go and have a look whats in the shed," said Nan.

They went out the back door and

down the garden. Nan squirted the WD40 into each padlock. They gave it a couple of minutes before trying to unlock the padlock. It was a bit stiff, but with a bit of working the key side to side, both locks were opened and they went inside. There was a strong smell of turpentine and spirit.

Jack held some of the work and looked at it, it was fantastic like nothing he had seen before. Jack felt inspiredand strong. He couldn't wait until next Saturday and the art class again. They spent the rest of the morning in there, going through the work, reading the notebooks and studying the sketchbooks of work yet to be done. Nan found her box of old newspapers. She opened it up and started to sort through the dfferent local, London and national papers that all had something about the death of

Jack's parents.

"Look at this. This is what I was getting at."

She handed the paper to Jack. The national paper headline said, 'Zapped: Anarchist scumbags sizzled out of existence', a London paper simply said, 'London 2: Anarchists 0'.

All of the papers then said that two anarchists had been killed whilst trying to vandalise a London tube train. The London paper had a photograph of one of the eye witnesses. He had a black leather jacket on and smart black trousers. The eye witness, a Mr Brown of Hampstead, was quoted as saying, "Yes, I was on my way home to my wife and young son, young St John Brown, when I was threatened by a pair of wild anarchists. They demanded money from me for their cause, before jumping onto the tracks to run over to carriage in the siddings to spray it. It was then that the Inter-City train hit them, poof. Red mist, all gone. On drugs no doubt. I felt tremendously sorry for them of course, but they needed to abide by the law like the rest of us."

Jack thought that Mr Brown's face looked familiar. The local paper was more sympathetic. Its headline read, 'Tragedy Befalls local family.' It went on to say, 'Local mother and father Charlie and Mille Love were believed to have been killed by an Inter-City train near Hackney Wick on Saturday night. They leave behind their only child Jack Love. It is understood that Jack is currently being cared for by his Grandmother, Shirley Spinks.

They spent hours look through the paperand eventually locked up the shed and went back inside.

Chapter 8

The week at school dragged by and there was no football training, too early for pre-season. Jack brought his Gola bag to school on Thursday for the art lesson. He wanted to asked Mr Burns about using a different paint with some of his brushes that he had at home. Mr Burns, was very pleased to help Jack, as he wanted him to do well in the competition.

Jack stayed for art club with Mr Burns after school for an hour.He walked across the St Barnaby playing fields as a short cut home. As he got near to the edge of the field where the old Mill Stream flowed before disappearing under the bridge and road on its way to the Roding, he saw a group of three older boys. They were fifth yearsand had just left school that day. That was them finished and out into the world. Jack recognised one of them as Tommy Grace, a boy whose name was like a sick joke across the school. The other two were the Webb twins. Grace was the school bully, taking lunch money, hurting children and being rude to teachers. Jack tried to avoid giving an eye contact at alland concentrated on walking as quickly as he could. But they had seen him and ran overand barred his way.

"What you got in the bag?" asked Grace.

"Nothing much," replied Jack quickening his pace.

Grace grabbed the bag and unzipped itand tipped out Jack's sketch books, paint brushes and the tube colours that Jack was showing Mr Burns.

"What a poof this kid is, look he's got brushes and all sorts in there. Do you do your nails with these brushes poof," shouted Grace.

"They are for my work."

"Work, painting work? What are you mental or a poof? Or a mental poof?" laughed Grace with what he thought was his menacing face.

The group of three boys, led by Grace, then started pushing Jack backward, towards the old Mill Stream until he was on the edge of it. Grace was holding Jack's paint brushes. He started snapping them one by and throwing them in the stream.

"The poof loves me, he loves me not," said Grace as he started to throw some of the brush halves into Jack's face.

Wayne and Darren Webb then pushed

Jack into the stream. Jack managed to steady himself so he didn't fall over, but his Solatios were now under water. This made Jack very annoyed, his mind throbbed with an electrical buzz.. He had worked hard to earn the money for those shoes. Grace now got to the remaining brush, which was wrapped in brown paper. He tipped the final brush out of the bagand looked at it as it lay on the grass. He hesitated a moment, as it looked a little different to the others. He then picked it upand almost instantaneously regretted it. His friends were still taunting Jackand not letting him scramble out of the stream. Each time he tried to make a break for it they pushed him back down the bankand into the water. Jack's feet were getting cold, even thought it was summer.

Grace screamed in pain. He was

crying in shock. Wayne and Darren had never heard Grace cry let alone scream. They stoppped in their tracks. The brush was searing a red hot scorch of heat into the hand of Grace. It was stuck there, burning into his hand, burning flesh. Wayne and Darren ran over and tried to help. But as they touched the brush to try and pull it away, they got burnt as well. Jack could see whatwas going on. He knew it was the brush his mother had given him. He walked instinctively over to the three boys and grabbed the brush out of Grace's hand, without any difficulty.

Grace fell onto the floor. He held his burnt right hand with his left. He tried to stretch his fingers. It was difficult because of the burn. But then he saw it. It wasn't a burn, but a branding. From the base of his little finger across his hand to his thumb was

a word, seared indelibly   C.O.W.A.R.D.
Grace screamed again, by not just in pain
this time, but in genuine, primitive fear. He
had seen the look on Jack's face. Wayne and
Darren made to go towards Jack to give him
a beating, as they thought him somehow
responsible, a trick of some kind. But then
they felt the same fearand shuddered to a
halt. They had seen something in Jack's eyes
which terrified them. Jack was holding the
brush and just starred at them. The three
boys, ran in the opposite direction, back
toward the school. Jack picked up his
bagand put everything back neatly in its
place. He would slowly dry his Solatios
when he got home, making sure the leather
soles didn't crack.

On Friday morning his classmates had
heard about him being attacked by the fifth

years. Jack had told no one. But in morning registration Susan Hill came over to him and asked if he was ok.

"Are you alright Jack. We've all heard about Grace coming after you. He left yesterday so he had nothing to lose. Is it true that him and the other two snapped all your brushes?" asked Susan.

"Well, they snapped nearly all of them, but its no bother Susan, honest,"said Jack.

"They are beasts those boys. Beasts," said Susan.

"Beasts are ok though."

At registration in the afternoon there was a knock on the form room door.

"Come in," said Mr Stevens who was the woodwork teacherand Jack's form tutor.

"Ah, Mr Burns, what can we do for

you?" said Mr Stevens.

Mr Burns was carrying a box.

"Susan, would you come out to the front please," asked Mr Burns, with a warm tone in his voice.

Susan did as she was told and went out to the front of the class and stood by Mr Steven's desk, next to Mr Burns.

"Here you are Susan, you can give this to him," asked Mr Burns.

"Jack, we all went to see Mr Burns and we gave the school our lunch money to buy these new brushes that Rowley and Newton rep had left for inspection. These are the best brushes we could get in the time. You deserve the best Jack. We all want you to paintand paint and paint, " said Susan.

Jack came out to receive his box. Jack looked at the faces of his class looking at himand he felt good.

"I don't know what to say. Thank you," smiled Jack, with a little bow.

Susan squeased his handand they all clapped him. Jack felt something new. He was happy. He liked Susan as well. That was a new feeling for him, liking girls.

"Well done Jack, what happened to Grace's hand,"asked Toby.

"I don't know," answered Jack, "some kind of burn."

Toby nodded, as if he understood the situation, which he didn't.

Chapter 9

Jack found it difficult sleeping that night. He kept thinking about Susanand her kindness toward him. He liked that very much. Saturday morning eventually arrived. Jack had his usual breakfast and then made his way to South Kensington on the tube. There had been signal trouble at Marble Arch, so Jack was forty minutes late.

When in the lobby Jack walked over to the board. A note pinned to the notice board said 'Professor Cringeworthy is sick and has been replaced for 'this week' by the notable (underlined) Maurice Bousenquet esq. OBE, RSA. Someone had added in pencil RSPCA, RAC, to complete the collection of letters after his name. When he finally arrived to the art class Jack made his way to his usual table and easel position. A short man with a bald head and a gaunt face, seemed to be calling a register, which hadn't been done before.

"Ah, I see. You have deemed to bless us with your presence I see, Jack is it?"

Jack started to say, "That's right I……………."

He was interupted.

"I don't really care who you are, but in my class you are to be here on time, do you hear," asserted Maurice Bosenquet with a flick of his head, as if tossing locks of hair which no longer existed. Fiona and the others were already there, dropped off by their parents in the usual high end cars. Crispin smirked as Jack started was being shouted at.

"Right, east end Jack here are three

hundred pencils, get 'em sharpened by breaktime and then you can THEN start the class," laughed Maurice Bosenquet in a false east end accent..

"There was trouble on the tube sir, it wasn't my fault," said Jack.

"It never is your kind's fault is it? With your fat bodies crammed into shiny track- suits, pushing kids in pushchairs around your filthy estates, 'fags' hanging out of your mouths, watching bloody Bullseye on your 'telly', Christ, you are a plebe," moaned Maurice Bosenquet.

Maurice Bosenquet grabbed Jack's bagand locked it in his cupboard.

"If you want your bag back, you'll do as I tell you, now get to work," that's Maurice Bosenquet OBE RCA telling you."
Maurice Bosenquet tapped his chest t further

indicate who he was talking about in case anyone had got lost! Frank walked into the room and heard the last of these words.

"Back off Bosenquet, he's just a kid, if you want to try and bully someone come and see me," said Frank.

"Oh, class solidarity, how touching, how quaint. Listen Frank 'me old son, me old mucker', your job's on the line as it is since Professor Not-worthy got the push. So if you want to keep earning your meagre sum to pay for your rabbit hutch out east you'd better button it," sneered Maurice Bosenquet.

Jack took the box and went out into the prep room, he sat there and started on the pencils. He had been given a penknife to do the job with, trimming the smallpieces of wood into a waste bin. Jack could hear that

Bosenquet had started to teach the class.

"Yes, I painted Leigh Bowery many times, more than Bacon or Freud. Freud used to say that I produced 'The Better Bowery', better than anyone elses, I captured what might be said to be the essential realisation of Bowery that wonderful performer. and today I am going to show you the technique that I used."
Maurice Bosenquet, expected some indication of reverenece from the students after hearing his words. He received none.

"What's the technique?" said Tarquin, "and I will get my tutor to run through it with me."

"That's wonderful Tarqs,"said said Maurice Bosenquet, as he daubed different paints from the different tubes right onto the canvas, "its called impastoand gives you texture and depth and looks like the paint is coming right out of the canvas. You can simply mix it there and then like this," said Maurice Bosenquet. The result, even to Tarquin looked like a complete mess.

"I see Maurice, I see,"said Tarquin, when it was clearly evident that he couldn't see.

"Can you see what it is yet?" asked Maurice Bosenquet, unconsciously borrowing a catchphrase from a TV artist.
There was silence in the class as Bosenquet whilred the paint around in what seemed a frenzy.

"Yes, well I think it may be a tree in Hyde Park?" suggested St John-Zedong.

"Close, close, its Buckingham Palace under assault from eastern hoardes," asserted Maurice Bosenquet with uncertain authority.

The class were set a task, to use the impasto technique to represent a form of cultural oppression. Tarquin immediately started painting a B29 Superfortess, which he said was the Enola Gay. St John-Zedong carried on the theme of 'western imperialism' with daubs paint representing B52s bombing Cambodia. Beatrice picked up on the theme and painted a picture of Field Marshall Mongomery wearing jack boots machine gunning miners 'in the north of England'. Fiona painted an abstract version of Richard Nixon where he had Saturn 5 rockets for legs and intercontinental balistic missles for arms. St John-Zedong seemed to both take offence at Fiona's workand find it very, very funny. He was unconsciously used to doublethink in his day to day life. Anything else was too stressful.

"Fiona old thing, doesn't your father work with Werhner Von Braun out at White Sands making rockets and the other accoutrements of western domination and mass destruction?" asked St John-Zedong.

"Listen you fake commie peasant, what papa does or doesn't do is none of your blasted business. Anyway your old man sells guns to the Africans and gets an OBE for it," laughed Fiona, pointing a pretend pistol at St John-Zedong.

"Class, class," said Bosenquet, "wonderful passion, wonderful. I hope you are capturing this lovely energy in your painting."

Jack joined the group after break and used his time to practice his use of Acrylics, in thick undiluted form.

He painted a scene from London Zoo, which was beautiful in its execution, but no more than that. Jack seemed to be holding himself in reserve. He felt depressed at these turn of events, with Cringeworthy goneand this new bloke in charge. On the way home that night Frank walked with Jack to the tube stationand sat next to him.

"Don't worry Jack, don't let them grind you down, you are made of better stuff than that," assured Frank, "you are going to produce something exceptional I know it."

"Thanks Frank, I am going to give it a real go. Lets see what happens."

They sat in silence the rest of the way home, with Jack getting off one stop before Frank. They were both deep in thought.

The following Saturday Maurice Bosenquet called the class around his teaching table at the front of the classand bade them sit on the stalls, before they left for the evening.

"As you know, next week we are taking part in the national painting competition, as part of the Princes' Art Class programme. The difference is that not only will there be a winning artist from one of the schools from Glasgow, Belfast, Leeds and west London, it will be on live television. The Prince and his team will be in a central studio, getting the live feed from the different schools and he will make his mind up and award the winning prize based on what he sees. This is the exciting big time, so make sure you areready next week," insructed Maurice Bosenquet.

When Jack left the building that evening he heard Fiona screaming at her father.

"Get me the head painter at the Slade round our place every night this week. I must have the best, because I must win. I am obviously the artist the Prince needs, but I want to make sure," screamed Fiona.

"You can't just buy people like servants," offered Fiona's father, which was a mistake that he regretted almost immediately.

"Yes you can. Mother said you basically bought herand you buy all those government contracts each year, you know the ones that you call your on 'your shopping list. You do it all the time, so buy me a painter."

"Tha.. that's different my darling Fiona, don't be saying that again," Fiona's father, looked nervously about in case any one was listening to him being bullied by his daughter.

"Number one. Do not presume to tell me what to do. Number two. I don't care, get the COW from the Slade sharpish," cried Fiona, "that bloody painter cow."

Jack heard similar 'conversations' going on with the other students as they got into their cars. He was almost invisible to them all now. They did not talk to him or acknowledge him in anyway.

Tarquin reached for a leg of turkey before he even reached the car, the driver was waving it out of his window. In between choking mouthfuls of roasted poultry Tarquin managed to say, "No, I don't want that bloody potter who puts words and rubbish on his pots, I want a proper artist, no not the tent one neither. Get me the guy who has the TV show on Saturday mornings, he knows how to win things. and win this Prince prize I shall. Get on with it."

Tarquin's father was audibly groaning in the seat of his sleek car. It was going to be an expensive week. Jack got the tube homeand kept himself to himself. No Frank this week. He missed him.

On Thursday morning, when Jack was walking to school he saw someone he recognised on a pushbike.

"Hello Frank," shouted Jack, "is that you?"

"Oh, hello Jack,"said Frank, pulling over to the kerb.

"Yes, I got the push from the art college. Old Bosenquet said I'd been nicking paintand selling it. He didn't like it that I stood up to him. But he knows people on the governing board of the collegeand that was that for old Frank," smiled Frank.

"That's a bit rough Frank, I am sorry if I've got you in trouble."

"It weren't you, it was old bald head's fault. Not you old son. You're a diamond. Anyway, every cloud etc. I've got an interview at the school up the road with a Mr Burns, head of art."

Jack smiled. Two good people together at his school!

"That's great Frank. That's my schooland I know Mr Burns he's my art teacherand he is very, very good," said Jack, "best of luck, I hope you get the job."

"Thanks Jack, I'll do my best and see where that gets me," said Frank.

That night Jack watched 'Top of the

Pops', he didn't really like it anymore but he watched anyhow. He thought the Paul MCartney song was a bit boringand he didn't like Leo Sayer at all. The only one singer he could listen to on the show was Kate Bush. He liked some of her songs. He thought she sounded a bit like the Minstrel, as she sang 'Babooshka'. Near the end of the show there was a ring on the door bell. Nan went to the door. Jack heard her talking through the door.

"Yes come in, I'll see if he would like to talk to you," Jack heard Nan say.

"Jack there's a man from the Ilford Record here. He wants to talk to you about the competition on Saturday, do you want to talk to him?"asked Nan.

The credits for Top of the Pops were rolling, so Jack said, "OK Nan. Send him through."

The man came into the front room and Nan asked him to sit down.

"I'm Nathan Selby, so Jack, have you met the Prince yet?"

"No, I've just been going to the classes."

"How did you get interested in artand painting?" asked Selby.

"Through my Nan. We paint animals and soldier models for a toy company, it came from that really."

Jack felt slightly uneay with this man. Nan was still in the room, but Jack sensed that this Selby had not got down to business, his real reason for being there yet.

"So you didn't inherit your mother and father's interest in art then. Have you seen these cuttings Jack," asked Selby as he laid out the same headlines he and Nan had looked at in the shed.

"I don't think so."

Nan had got up from the end of the room and was walking towards Selby, with a protective look in her eye.

"They were criminals Jack, vandals who were killed spraying a tube train. How do you feel about that?" asked Selby raising his voice, as he laid his hand on Jack's shoulder in an attempt to intimidate or sympathise, Selby wasn't sure what it was, but it usually worked on the great unwashed public. Selby would regret that action. As Selby laid his hand on Jack's shoulder, Jack had a vision and an insight as clear as the Kate Bush video.

"You never reported the hit and run you did in Barkingside High Street last year,

did you, its eating you up, give yourself up,"
stated Jack in a matter of fact tone looking
directly into Selby's face.

Nan stood still. Selby, went pale. He almost
seemed to choke. He got up and staggered to
the front door, leaving his notepad,
newpaper cuttings and his bag. He opened
the door and ran up the path, not closing it
behind him.

"What did you say to him?" asked
Nan.

"I don't know Nan, I just had a
picture in my mindand now he's gone."

Nan didn't labour the point, but she
had seen something that had disturbed her.
Something extremely powerful.

Chapter 10

It was Saturday morning. The day. A crowd had gathered at South Kensington Station as Jack merged from the underground. As Jack walked along with his Gola bag the crowd followed him. There was a picture of him on the newspaper stand by the station entrance.

Someone shouted, "Go on Jack, show'em 'ow to paint."

Another voice shouted, "We're with you Jack, we all think you're great."

As he turned the final corner Jack couldsee all the TV outside broadcasting cables running in through the front doorand he could see Keith Candice the TV man talking into the camera as he got near the door.

He could hear Keith say, "and here he comes now, the orphan from the east, maaaaaaaa - ster Jack Love."

Jack found the microphone in front of him and the TV camera. Keith was blocking the way so he had to stop walking. Jack couldn't stand being in the crowd that had now gathered. Big crowds and noise had that affect on him. It made him feel woozy and uneasy. He wanted to put his hands over his ears, like he used to do. His vision seemed to narrow and his hearing was almost like listening down a tunnel, kind of like hearing distant echoes.

"So Jack you're not wearing your trade mark Solatios today Jack, whats afoot as they say?" asked Keith.

Jack simply replied, "No."

"What will you paint today Jack, we

hear that you are really good. Will it be a street scene from the east end of London, a big double decker bus, a Pearly King and Queen, Walthamstow Market, what have you got up your sleeve?" asked Keith without irony.

The camera light was shinning right into Jack's eyesand it was hurting himand giving him a headache.

"I will do my best and paint the truth," answered Jack.

There was panic on Keith's faceand fear of not understanding. This clearly wasn't an answer that Keith was expectingand he stepped back to gather his thoughts and look at his notes. As Keith did that, Jack side stepped him like he did against Formaldyhyde Tyke. Past and through. It was a little quieter inside the building. Jack walked to his normal table and easel. Maurice Bosenquet was in his element. He was wearing a bright bow tie, yellow shirt, blue blazer and cream trousers. His head seemed to have been polished and had the appearance of a snooker ball. A camera was already sey up for an establishing shot in the room, for the group meeting before they started on their painting. As Jack walked in the talking all stoppedand they looked at him as one.

"We have had brilliant preparation Jack, all of us, because we are successful and you're not. Go 'home' to your hovel now. The Prince will pick one of usand probably will use all of us for his portrature and landscapes over the years to come anyway. Its not going to be The Prince and the Pauper this time, so you may as well go," threatened Fiona, but there was a nervousness in her voice that Jack had not heard before.

Beatrice chimed in with, "I know what prep he did. Eating fish and chips with his bloody Nan. That's what he does. What a plebe."

They all laughed, one more time at his expense. Bosenquet called the morning meeting around the central table. As the camera lense went in on the hate filled mocking jealous faces were transformed, now all was smilesand thank yous and after yousand kindness was spread by each candidate in front of the camera.

Keith Candice was now in the studio directing the filming and interviewing the young artists.

Fiona spoke directly to the camera,

"Its so wonderful that Jack is here with us. Art can sometimes seem like an unecessary luxury when you are on the bread line, so its great that the country sees how all talent is recognised in our wonderful meritocracy."

Fiona had been also taking media classes as well as art tuition, with the same agency that the government used, Spandy and Spandy. They had made her speak slowerand to lower her eyes a little when speaking to camera and to soften her voice. Which they had told her, told her! Was shrill.

Keith Candice had made his way around the room. He now said, "The artists will now all make their way to their tables and equipment, just as our candidates from Belfast, Glasgow and Leeds are now doing around the country. Whats it like in Belfast Maureen?"

"Oh, we will give you a strong competition from Belfast so we will. They are painting with a vim and a spirit that will catch the Prince's eye I am sure," assured Maureen.

Keith smiled, a glazed eye smile for the camera.

"Come in Glasgow, Come in Glasgow, are you there Bill?" said Keith.

"Bill Turner here, broadcasting from the Central School in Princes Street. and with the quality of young artists that have been assembled here, this will be the 'Street' that the Prince selects his champion painter from."

"Thank you Bill. They may be streets ahead in Glasgow but whats the state of play with you Stacey Finch in Leeds, coming from the Headingly cricket ground pavillion?" asked Keith.

"Tremendous energy here Keith. Each artist has consumed a full English Breakfast in the Yorkshire canteen, with a full pint of Yorkshire tea. Its simply a marvelous pick-me-up for any artist of worth. Crispy bacon, crispy art, full of calories and taste. Just like our artists. N't that right," asked Stacey to the crowd of young artists.

The outside broadcast microphones picked up a kind of groan from the roomand a scraping or plates and that of chairs being moved about. It then went blank, no sound or vision.

"A big thank you to Stacey in Leeds. Whata wonderful sight, wonderful. We will be making a visit back to each studio for the judging late this afternoon. Back to you, Hugh, in the studio," said Keith.

As soon as the camera was off, Keith stormed over to Jack and shouted, "Hey, boy, don't you make me look bloody stupid again you got it, painting the truth, you bloody little fool?"

Jack turned and looked at him with a genuine surprise, he could n't place why this man should be annoyed. Keith was used to 'reading' his intervieweesand there was something he saw in Jack's eyes which made him stop and back off. He'd seen that look somewhere before, but he could n't place it. Either way, it made him move off quickly.

Each of the young west London artists had prepared in detail for this moment. It was the most concentrated that any of them had been in their lives. The canvasses were being carefilly laid out using a variety of media, as part of the step by step process each had been tutored for.

Tarquin used a roller to seal the blank canvass in an off-white paint wash. Charcoal was being painstakingly used by Crispin and St John-Zedong to lay out their paintings. Beatrice had decided on pastels for this stage of her work. Mark Anthony her tutor had told her it would give her the edge with speed. Bosenquet was wandering around the studio in a self-important haze.

Unfortunately he had not accounted for Fiona's new impasto technique, a technique which after all, he the great maestro of the easel had introduced to her. The thick layers of paint were not the trouble for Bosenquet. The issue, which required the use of the art school's First Aid Box, was Fiona's paint knife arm's considerable backlift. As

Bosenquet lent in for a look at the Fiona's work her pallet knife slashed backwards, just nicking his chin. A combination of events amplified the effect of this minor injury. Keith was directing the camera to film some background footage, which could be used under credits or voice overs and caught the incident full square into the lens. Fiona was daubing her most expensive bright crimson heavily from her knife. When the blade just touched Bosenquet's chin, the red paint transfer was seamless to the untrained eye. Bosenquet, seeing what he believed to be a slash wound requiring at least fifty A & E stitches went into a frenzy of self pity an panick.

He screamed, on camera, "She's done for me! This vile girl has disfigured me for life, my beauty has been rendered asunder. I shall never recover, never."

Fiona seeing the confusion found the incident, extremely funny.

She laughed and said, "Oh no, poor Bosenquet has copped a Blighty one, call for the medics."

Keith couldn't believe his luck with this footage. A few stills from the film should be worth a few bob to the Sunday papers, his favourite being 'The Sunday Sluice', he loved the Sluice, cleaning up them that needed cleaning up, wonderful and change in his pocket for the pictures as well. He made a mental note to have a quiet word with the camera man on the mutually beneficial business. One of the art school's other tutors brought a clean damp cloth and wiped Bosenquet's face. No cut could even been seen. He sat on a stool in the middle of the room with his lovely yellow shirt ruined with red paint. Inwardly he was fuming. Composure, composure, he told himself. One must keep one's decorum at all costs. He took a deep breath got up from his stool and continued his walk, as if nothing had happened.

Through all of this commotion Jack sat by his table, deep in thought. It was 10.45 a.m. now, tea break timeand Jack had not started, not even a single stroke of the brush or graze of charcoal onto his canvass. No one was paying any heed to him though. They were all too busy with their own masterpieces to notice. and masterpieces they must surely be with the amount of money spent on paints and brushes. Crispin's paintbox was a cantilevered work of art in itself, made of the finest veneer marquetry, he was very busy with his palette. He looked over for a moment and saw Jack motionless. For a second he was slightly worried, but then his tactical mind took overand he thought good, one less competitor for me to beat. The law of the jungle and all that. The students gathered around the main central table for their tea break, leaving Jack on his own. Each had brought their own tuck box.

"Look, the suburban loser, hasn't even started. No fibre, no backbone those types, when the chips are down, maybe that's the trouble insufficient chips down, having fish 'n' chip withdrawl symptoms no doubt," laughed Fiona sarcasticlly.

"Maybe we should all start singing one of those football songs, like the plebes do, to wake the silly so-and-so upand make him feel at home, he's probably thirsty, someone make him a Bovril," laughed St John-Zedong.

The others joined in the laughter. But Jack sat immobile. He heard none of this. He found himself stand up now, as the others made their way back to their canvasses. He slowly walked past them all lookingand not looking at their work. Hearingand not hearing their spiteful comments to himand to each other. Their was an empty, meaningless hate eminating from the group of young artists.

Jack knew that these young people had every material thing that they could possibly want but were still deeply unhappy. It seemed to Jack that they had somehow chosen to be this way, chosing hateand jealously. They were creating a hateful world which was eating them upand they were doing it to themselves. Jack felt their pointless pain as he walked through the studio. The young artists' words of hateand sarcasm may be directed at others but it was to themselves that they were talkingand that hurt Jack, to think such a thing possible. Such a waste. Jack carried on walking, out of the studio, down the corridorand out into the light. He wanted a breather to gather his thoughts. He had been trying to decide whether to use 'the brush', the one he had brought back, or not. It was in its brown paper wrapping sitting on his table. He felt both exhilerated and worried about using it. He had pushed thinking about the jungle to the back of his mind, but now he had to confront it. He turned and walked back to the studio.

St John was producing a Fruedianesque nude, very well painted but highly derrivative. He had made six of the same painting at home being drilled by his spindly tutor. Fiona's impasto abstract was also clearly well practised, but was a seventh rate Picasso still life, dominated by an eye singeing red. The paint was an inch thick in places. St John-Zedong true to his 'beliefs' and support of the suppressed north Vietnamsese was painting a Le Pho lookalike effort, complete with B52s bombing the jungle with MAD comics. Tarquin's painting looked like stripy wall paper, but his confident smirk told everyone that he thought it was his masterpiece on a par with Barnett Newman. Beatrice was dressed today as usual as a Mediterranean peasant. She daubed paint to form the large and heavy Georgia O'Keefe that she had been copying at home.

Jack was back at his table. He fumbled the wrapping paper for a moment, but he then had the brush in his hand. Jack began to paint with his new brush. His movements were very, very swift, almost beyond belief in their intensity. Keith Candice was in the process of getting his makeup done. He was about to go back on air. He saw Jack start his work.

The floor manager said, "Keith, the other studios are ready, they've got twenty minutes and then the cameras will do a walk round and the Prince will make his choice. We are going last, as the word is the winner is coming out of here."

Bosanquet shouted "Last twenty minutes now, last twenty minutes. He started a slow walk around the canvasses. Keith smirked, "Come along artists put your best brush forward, time is running out."

Jack was now painting with a fury and speed no one had seen from him before, it was astonishing in its power.

In the central studio the Prince and his advisers had gathered around the specially arranged monitor. They were ready for the camera walk through. Bosanquet had continued his walk around the studio. The work was very competent he thought. Bosanquet finally came to Jack's paining. He stopped in fear and bewilderment by Jack's painting.

Jack's competitors one by one became aware that Bosanquet was no longer hovering around them, advising and guiding, but by that bloody Jack. The bloody plebe.

He was taking their time!

Fiona shouted, "Bosanquet, you've not gone all Cringeworthy on us have you, helping the poor boy Jack? We got rid of him, come over here and help me, not the suburban plebe."

Bosanquet remained transfixed where he was, looking at Jack's painting and wasn't that a slight tremor in his lip, the camera would pick that up. Hearing, Fiona fail all the other 'artists' called Bosanquet over to help them.

Tarquin shouted, "Come on Bosanquet, set to." Still no movement!

One by one they called out their protests. They asked what he is playing at and that he should be giving them his time, not the suburban loser, as they call Jack. Bosanquet did not answer them either.

Unease started to sit with the young artists.

'Keith, they're doing the Belfast walk through now," shouted the floor manager urgently into Keith's earpiece.

In the central studio the Prince's team were being shown a good strong selection of paintings from Belfast.

"I like that one," said the Prince to his adviser, pointing at the screen indicating a nice landscape painting of Dunluce Castle.

"Rupert, let's see that last one again will you?" asked the adviser to the Belfast team. The Prince had a good look at the castle again. He liked it, tapping the screen with his pen. The Leeds studio had some really talented young artists. One of them had painted Leeds United in full flow at Elland Road. It was quite brilliant. It even had Don Revie in it. The Prince chose that one from the Leeds bunch. The Glasgow art was fantastic. There was a huge range of styles and abilities. The energy was real. It was authentic, which the Prince could see. He carried over three from Glasgow.

In the west London studio Tarquin, St John-Zedong, Beatrice, Crispin and eventually Fiona, almost against her will were all drawn to look at Jack's painting. As they made their way towards Jack's canvass they saw that Bosanquet was now lying quite still on the floor.

"What's that bloody Bosanquet doing Keith, sort him out will you, we are going live in 3, 2, 1, we're live Keith," shouted the floor manager.

The camera was now slowly going past each painting, pausing for a minute and then moving on. The Prince was disappointed. He thought the originality and standard would be much higher, but all he could see were works that looked like someone else's, something he had seen before. Keith was following the camera around and trying to give some commentary to each work, with one eye on Bosanquet on the floor still.

"St John-Zedong has produced a wonderful reflective piece………….," Keith started, but was cut off by his floor manager.

"The Prince wants you to shut up Keith," instructed the floor manager.

The west London young artists were each now gathered around Jack's painting. Each in turn, with glazed and fearful eyes, laid down on the parquet floor. A 'traumatic trance', a phrase that was coined some time after, had taken over these students. Taken over and stunned them. The power, intensity and searing truth of Jack's painting had affected everyone who saw it. Some were transfixed, other felt a rush of elation. All were overwhelmed. Each saw a truth, a truth about them which was like an earthquake in their mind, in their soul. They saw in that moment, what they had done to themselves, the mutations and distortions that they had become and the hate that they embodied. It was an instantaneous realisation both horrific and beautiful at the same time. Jack's work had been painted with all the qualities he had proved in the jungle.

The TV camera then arrived, for the national live hook up, in front of Jack's painting. Nan was watching at home, live on BBC1.

When Jack's painting was shown into

the camera the Prince was looking at on his monitor. The Prince said automatically to his adviser, "That is the one. That's the overall winner."

As the Prince said these words, Keith and the floor manager both heard his decision. Then something happened. The camera feed went blank and all of the broadcasting was shut down. It was as if lightening had struck the cables and blown all the fuses. Keith and the floor manager looked each other and then it was over.

When Jack got home and told his Nan, she smiled and said, "I knew that you would win Jack, but the tiger told me you were certain to win."

Printed in Great Britain
by Amazon